RITA HERRON

BENEATH the BADGE

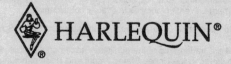

HARLEQUIN®

TORONTO • NEW YORK • LONDON
AMSTERDAM • PARIS • SYDNEY • HAMBURG
STOCKHOLM • ATHENS • TOKYO • MILAN • MADRID
PRAGUE • WARSAW • BUDAPEST • AUCKLAND

To Rickey and Delores for making me fall in love
with the Rangers....

ISBN-13: 978-0-373-69348-1
ISBN-10:   0-373-69348-6

BENEATH THE BADGE

www.eHarlequin.com

Printed in U.S.A.

HARLEQUIN®

INTRIGUE®

COMING NEXT MONTH

INTRIGUE'S ULTIMATE HEROES
★

#1083 MONTANA ROYALTY by B.J. Daniels
Whitehorse, Montana
Devlin Barrow wasn't like any cowboy Rory Buchanan had ever rode with. The European stud brought status to her ranch—as well as a trail of assassins and royal intrigue.

#1084 BODYGUARD TO THE BRIDE by Dani Sinclair
Xavier Drake had been on difficult missions before, but none more challenging than posing as Zoe Linden's bodyguard. Once he got his hands on the pregnant bride, it would be tough giving her away.

#1085 SHEIK PROTECTOR by Dana Marton
Karim Abdullah was the most honorable sheik and the fiercest warrior throughout the desert kingdom. On his word he vowed to protect Julia Gardner and her unborn child—the future prince of his war-torn land.

#1086 SOLVING THE MYSTERIOUS STRANGER
by Mallory Kane
The Curse of Raven's Cliff
The fortune told of a dark and mysterious stranger who had the power to save Raven's Cliff. But could Cole Robinson do it without sacrificing the town's favorite daughter, Amelia Hopkins?

#1087 SECRET AGENT, SECRET FATHER by Donna Young
Jacob Lomax awoke with no memory and an overpowering instinct for survival. In a race against time, the secret agent had to reconstruct the last twenty-four hours of his life, if he was to save Grace Renne and the unborn child that may be his.

#1088 COWBOY ALIBI by Paula Graves
Tough, embittered Wyoming police chief Joe Garrison had one goal: finding the person responsible for his brother's murder. But when a beautiful amnesiac Jane Doe surfaced in need of his help, his quest for justice turned into the fight of their lives.

ABOUT THE AUTHOR

Award-winning author Rita Herron wrote her first book when she was twelve, but didn't think real people grew up to be writers. Now she writes so she doesn't have to get a *real* job. A former kindergarten teacher and workshop leader, she traded her storytelling to kids for romance, and writes romantic comedies and romantic suspense. She lives in Georgia with her own romance hero and three kids. She loves to hear from readers so please write her at P.O. Box 921225, Norcross, GA 30092-1225, or visit her Web site at www.ritaherron.com.

Books by Rita Herron

CAST OF CHARACTERS

Sgt. Hayes Keller—This tough ranger resents the rich, especially Taylor Landis, the heiress he is forced to protect. So why does his blood run hot around her?

Taylor Landis—When a killer targets her, she must accept protection from the surly Sergeant Hayes Keller. But she absolutely won't get involved with the man....

Lt. Brody McQuade—Head of the rangers' Unsolved Crimes Unit, he wants to capture the villain terrorizing Cantara Hills and see that justice is done.

Sgt. Egan Caldwell—The Texas Ranger is eager to close the case in Cantara Hills before anyone else falls prey to an elusive killer.

Miles Landis—He wants his sister's money—would he kill for it?

Margaret Hathaway—Could her secret have something to do with the attacks on Taylor?

Link Hathaway—Margaret's powerful father forced her to give up her child years ago; is he working behind the scenes now to keep them apart?

Devon Goldenrod—Margaret's fiancé will do anything to beat Kenneth Sutton and keep Margaret—would he kill to get what he wants?

Walt Caldwell—How far does Egan's father's loyalty to Link Hathaway stretch?

Kenneth Sutton—He's running for governor—would he kill to protect his campaign?

Tammy Sutton—Kenneth's wife will do anything to keep her husband and herself in the spotlight.

Chapter One

"Taylor Landis needs protection."

Sergeant Hayes Keller pushed his half-eaten blood-red steak away, his appetite vanishing. He knew Brody McQuade, his lieutenant, was still pissed at him for sleeping with his sister, Kimberly, and forcing him to *babysit* the richest, prissiest heiress in Texas must be his way of punishing him.

"But Montoya killed Kimberly," Hayes said, "and Carlson tried to kill Caroline, and you took care of him."

Brody cleared his throat. "We have to tie up loose ends. I'm at the crime lab in Austin, and we got the results of Carlson's autopsy. Egan said Carlson acted as if he'd been drugged, and the coroner found ketamine in his system."

"Ketamine—that's Special K on the streets. I'm not surprised," Hayes said. "Carlson had money. He ran with the party crowd."

Brody sighed, sounding weary. "We need to search Carlson's place, see if we find evidence of the drug."

"Why? He's dead. Good riddance."

"Yeah. But during the shoot-out, when Egan confronted Carlson about being on drugs, he denied taking anything."

"So you think someone else drugged him?"

"That's what I want to know."

Hell. He wouldn't be at all surprised that someone else wanted Carlson dead.

"And we still aren't sure who planted that bomb that blew up Taylor's car. It looks as if it was intended for her, not for Caroline. Which means that if Carlson tried to kidnap Caroline because she had him fired and he didn't commit all these murders, someone else wanted to hurt Taylor."

"So she's still in danger." Hayes slapped his beer down on the bar. He so wanted this case to be over, so he could leave Cantara Hills. "Carlson probably set the bomb."

"Maybe, maybe not. Caroline is worried sick about Taylor. She said that Taylor admitted that Kimberly and Kenneth Sutton had argued before the hit-and-run. I want to know what that argument was about."

Damn. Kenneth Sutton—the powerful and ambitious chairman of the City Board who was now running for governor. Kimberly had been interning in the man's office before her murder.

And she *had* been upset about something that had happened with the board, that was the reason Hayes had been comforting her the night they'd ended up in bed. Although she'd refused to confide the reason.

Brody was right. They had to tie up every unanswered question. He owed Brody, and he owed Kimberly.

The waitress glanced at his beer to see if he wanted a refill. He did, but he shook his head and indicated he needed the check. Duty called.

"So who would want to hurt Taylor Landis?"

Brody grunted. "That's what you need to find out. Could be related to her family's foundation, or Sutton's hiding something." Brody hesitated. "Miles Landis is also suspect."

Miles, Taylor's half brother. The snotty brat had rubbed him wrong the moment he'd met him. "Yeah, I heard he's had money troubles."

"Right. And Taylor is supposed to inherit a boatload of money in four weeks, on her thirtieth birthday," Brody continued. "That's motive for Miles."

Hayes grabbed the check and tossed down some cash, then strode toward the door. Tonight he'd wanted to drown himself in cheap beer, listen to country music and hang with the real people.

Instead, he had to head back to the neighborhood of the rich and greedy and Taylor Landis.

COULD THIS DAY GET ANY WORSE?

First the confrontation with Kenneth regarding his possible tampering with the bid for the new city library, then that ordeal with Miles at the restaurant.

The only highlight was the excitement about her best friend Margaret Hathaway's upcoming wedding. Margaret had been alone a long time, had never gotten over giving her son up for adoption when she was fifteen. She'd even hinted at hiring a P.I. to look for him, but her father, Link, had insisted against it. Poor Margaret. Her friend's pain had prompted Taylor to hire the P.I.

herself. Finding out that her son's adopted family loved him would make a perfect wedding gift to Margaret. Then she could finally have the happiness she deserved.

Her cell phone rang, and she checked the number as she turned into Cantara Hills. Miles.

Not again.

She let it ring until it went to voice mail, but a second later, it started all over again. Knowing he wouldn't give up, she hit the connect button.

"I knew you were there," Miles snarled.

"Listen, I already told you that I'm not giving you any money right now. Grow up and start being responsible."

"You'll be sorry for turning your back on me, Taylor."

A chill swept up Taylor's spine. "Is that a threat?"

His bitter laugh echoed over the line. "It's a promise."

The dial tone buzzed in her ear as he abruptly ended the call.

Taylor shivered. After her mother's death, her father had quickly remarried. But his marriage to Miles's mother hadn't lasted long, and both she and Miles had been bitter and had tried repeatedly to milk him for money. But she'd never heard Miles so out of control. As she pulled down the drive to her mansion, she saw the crime scene tape in her driveway, and her senses jumped to alert.

The tape and the smoky, charred debris that had stained the imported Italian brick reminded her that someone had tried to kill her. That her body parts, instead of her BMW's, could have been all over the lawn....

If she hadn't rescheduled her appointment, she

would have been driving home at the time the bomb exploded. According to Sergeant Egan Caldwell, the device had been set on a timer. Which meant that someone had known her routine and had intentionally planned for the car to explode with her inside.

Could Miles have done it? Or was Carlson Woodward responsible?

But why would Carlson have wanted her dead?

Hugging her arms around herself, she scanned the front of her estate, feeling paranoid as she let herself in and checked her security system. Ever since the break-ins had started in Cantara Hills, she'd been nervous. Had expected to be hit. After all, her mansion held expensive furniture, paintings, vases, collectibles, and she had several exquisite customized one-of-a-kind pieces of jewelry her father had given her over the years.

All tucked away in her safe because she rarely wore them. She enjoyed the advantages money offered, but didn't flaunt her wealth. In fact, that money was sometimes a curse. While most girls had to worry about men wanting in their pants, she had the added hassle of wondering if they wanted to get into her bank account. Even her father used his wealth to replace his feelings for her with expensive gifts.

And the break-ins—did the police believe that Carlson Woodward was responsible for them? She frowned and walked through the kitchen to the foyer and the spiral staircase, then wound her way up to her suite.

But why would Carlson steal from the neighbors? He didn't need the money. Her little brother, Miles, was a different story. He was so desperate for cash and angry with some of her friends who'd begun refusing him loans, that he might resort to theft.

She slipped into a bathing suit, sighing as her bare feet sank into the plush Oriental rug. Padding barefoot down the steps, she exited through the sunroom, grabbed a towel from the pool house and dropped it, along with her cell phone, onto a patio chair. The last vestiges of sunlight had faded hours ago, but the pool lights illuminated the terrace, bathing the intricately patterned stonework in a pale glow. The smell of roses from the garden along with hydrangeas bordering the patio scented the air, disguising the hint of chlorine, and she stared into the shimmering aquamarine water.

Still, thoughts of Carlson's attack on Caroline haunted her. She and Caroline had been neighbors and friends for years now. Apparently, Carlson had spread rumors in the community about Caroline having an affair with Sergeant Egan Caldwell, and had even called her father to stir up trouble.

Then he had attacked Caroline. Thankfully Ranger Caldwell had rescued Caroline and shot Carlson. Unfortunately Egan had been injured in the confrontation. Now Caroline had accompanied him to Austin to take care of him while he recuperated. Taylor still couldn't believe that Caroline had fallen for the surly ranger.

She dove into the water and began a crawl stroke. She and Caroline had joked about the three cowboy cops who'd invaded their country club community with their big bodies, hard attitudes and...guns. They'd dubbed Lieutenant Brody McQuade, Kimberly's brother, the intense one. Sergeant Egan Caldwell, the surly one. And Sergeant Hayes Keller—he had a chip on his shoulder the size of Texas.

Still, an odd tingling rippled through her as she thought about him—he was all bad attitude. Big, brawny, muscular, with eyes as black as soot and a temper as hot as fire. He was just the kind of man she normally avoided because he looked as if he could snap a person into pieces with just one look. But still, he was dangerously sexy....

Her stomach clenched. Where had that thought come from?

She didn't even like the guy. When he'd questioned her, she'd felt his disdain carving a hole through her.

She'd be glad when he left the area.

She swam another lap, counting strokes, but suddenly the lights flickered off, both outside and inside, pitching the terrace into darkness. Her breath hitched. There wasn't a storm cloud in sight, no reason for a power failure.

Something was wrong.

Scanning the terrace and garden for signs of an intruder, she swam to the pool edge to get out and call security. Suddenly a movement at the edge of the gardens by the pool house caught her eye.

A man?

Panic shot through her. She had to call for help. But the chair where she'd put her phone was next to the gardens.

And the only unlocked door was the sunroom door. She'd have to pass the pool house to reach it.

Taking a deep breath, she took off running, but before she reached the door, someone clamped a gloved hand over her mouth and encircled her neck with the other.

She clawed at his hands, but he dug his fingers into her larynx, cutting off her air. Remembering the self-defense moves she'd learned, she jabbed her elbow in his chest, brought her knee up then stomped down on his foot.

He growled in fury and tightened both hands around her throat. Blind panic assaulted her. She couldn't breathe, couldn't see. Desperate, she reached for something to use as a weapon as they fell against a patio chair. Her hand closed around a garden shovel and she stabbed backward with it, but he knocked it from her hand and it skittered across the terrace.

Enraged, he punched her jaw so hard her ears rang and she saw stars.

She had to fight back. But he hit her again, her legs buckled and her knees hit the stone with a painful thud. He shoved her face down, and she tasted blood as her head slammed against the brick wall encircling the patio. Then he dragged her toward the pool.

Summoning her last bit of strength, she flailed and kicked, clawed at him, but they tumbled into the pool.

Gasping, she struggled to fight her way back to the surface, but he was too strong. She held her breath, but her lungs were on fire, and he squeezed her throat so tightly that she choked and inhaled water.

Then an empty darkness sucked her into its vortex.

HAYES PULLED TO A STOP at the iron-gated entrance to Taylor Landis's estate, and pressed the intercom button. He tapped his fingers on the steering wheel as he waited, but she didn't respond. Dammit, even if she wasn't home, didn't she have servants at her beck and call day and night?

He pressed the call button again, his impatience growing. What the hell was she doing? Lounging in some hot bath with cucumbers over her eyes, sipping champagne? Entertaining one of her rich guy friends? Maybe they were wallowing in bed with all their money.

Hell, maybe she wasn't home. Probably out shopping.

Still, he had to make sure she was safe. Resigned, he scanned the key card through the security system. But the card didn't work. Dammit, had she changed the system without informing them?

Or could something be wrong?

His heartbeat slammed in his chest, and he climbed out, removed his weapon, vaulted over the fence and jogged through the oaks lining the mile-long driveway, scanning the property for an intruder.

As the house slid into view, he searched the front yard, the sign of the crime scene tape a reminder that Brody might be right—that Taylor Landis might be in danger. He sped up until he reached the house, a cold monstrosity made of stone and brick with arches and palladium windows.

The hair on the back of his neck prickled. Why were the lights off?

The lingering odor of smoke and charred grass assaulted him, and he paused, a noise breaking the quiet. Water? A sprinkler maybe? But it had rained last night so why would Taylor have the sprinkler on?

He hurried to the front door and rang the doorbell. The sound reverberated through the cavernous inside, an empty sound that came unanswered. He pressed it again, then glanced through a front window. Nothing looked out of place. But it was pitch-dark inside. Quiet.

No movement. And there hadn't been a storm to knock out the power.

What if someone had disarmed Taylor's security or cut her lights?

Another noise jarred him, and he jerked his head toward the side of the house, then realized the noise had come from the back.

Sucking in a breath, he wielded his gun and slowly inched along the length of the house to the side, then around the corner where a terrace held a pool, sitting area, fireplace, cooking pit and a pool house. A clay flowerpot was overturned, dirt spilled across the stone.

Senses alert, his gaze swept the perimeter and the gardens. A water hose lay on the ground, spraying the stone. He shut off the water, wondering why someone would have directed it toward the pool instead of the lawn.

His breath caught as he neared the pool. A body was floating facedown inside.

God.

It was Taylor Landis.

Chapter Two

Heart pounding, Hayes laid his gun beside the pool, threw off his Stetson and boots, then dove into the water. He flipped Taylor over, cursing at the bruises on her face and neck as he carried her up the steps. Her long blond hair was a tangled mass around her slender face, and her arms dangled beside her, limp and lifeless.

He eased her onto one of the pool chairs, guilt nagging him for thinking that she'd been out shopping while she'd obviously been struggling for her life.

He quickly checked for a pulse. Hell, he couldn't find one.

He punched the number for security. "Taylor Landis was assaulted. I need an ambulance and CSI team ASAP, and have your people search the surrounding area!"

He disconnected the call, then started chest compressions, tilted her head back, gently moved aside her hair, pinched her nose and began mouth-to-mouth resuscitation. "Come on, Taylor, breathe."

Instead, she lay as limp as a rag doll, deathly pale.

Sweat exploded across his brow as he continued CPR.

Another breath. More chest compressions. Sirens wailed in the distance, coming closer. "Come on, Taylor, don't die on me. Fight, dammit."

He inhaled, closed his lips over hers again, and said a silent prayer that he hadn't lost her already. Suddenly her body jerked and she gasped, a strangled plea for air. She was alive....

He muttered a silent thanks as he watched her eyes flicker.

She coughed, choking and gulping in air, and he tilted her head sideways so she could release the excess water trapped in her lungs. Her body trembled, then she slowly opened her eyes and her terrorized gaze met his.

Did she remember what had happened? Could she identify her attacker?

TAYLOR SHIVERED, CLAWING her way through the darkness. She was cold and shaking and ached all over. And she was so weak... What had happened?

Muddied, terrifying memories crashed back and panic bolted through her. The pool...the attack...she'd been fighting off the man, but he'd pushed her under water...

She had almost died.

A strangled cry escaped her, and she blinked to clear her vision, then stared in confusion at the man above her.

Sergeant Hayes Keller.

His black eyes pierced her like lasers, while his hands gripped her by the shoulders. For a brief moment, fear seized her, but he stroked her cheek so gently that a tidal wave of emotions welled inside her and tears flowed down her face.

"Shh, you're going to be all right now, Taylor. I've called an ambulance."

She gave a slight nod, then swallowed hard to stifle another cry, but the pitiful sound came out anyway. Embarrassed, she pressed her hand over her eyes to regain control and shield herself from his probing look.

She hated to appear weak in front of anyone. Especially this big tough guy with the bad attitude. He didn't like her, and she didn't like him.

"Are you hurt anywhere?" He lifted her fingers from her face, his voice husky and low.

"I'm…okay," she whispered, although her throat felt raw and her voice sounded strained and broken. The effort it took for her to talk triggered a coughing spell, and he lifted her at an angle, murmuring comforting words until the fit subsided, and she sagged back against him.

"Taylor, did you see your attacker? Do you know who did this?"

She shook her head. "Too dark…"

"Was he on foot? Did you hear a car?"

"I don't know." An involuntary shudder rocked her. "He jumped me from behind…."

He clenched his jaw, looking harsh, yet his hands were tender as he stroked her back. "Just relax," he said. "Let me get you a towel or something."

He eased her back down on the chair, and she clutched his arm, not wanting him to leave.

"I'll be right back." He rushed away but returned in seconds and wrapped a thick, plush bath towel around her.

"I need to open the gate for the ambulance," he said. "The security system was off and I couldn't get through."

She frowned, then realized that her attacker must have disarmed the alarm. But when? And how?

"Inside," she said in a ragged voice. "By the mudroom entrance."

He nodded, raced to the side entrance then disappeared inside the house. Terrified that her attacker might still be lurking nearby, she glanced around the terrace. There hadn't been a car in the drive when she'd arrived home. And she hadn't heard one after she went in the house. He must have come in on foot.

The rose garden with its canopy of trees, bushes and elaborate labyrinth of flower beds normally looked inviting but now it seemed eerie, a place for an intruder to hide. Even her home with its fortress of rooms would provide cover. He could be in a closet or one of the extra suites or even in her bedroom, for that matter.

Another chill swept through her.

What if her attacker was inside? What if he killed the ranger, then returned to finish her off?

HAYES HAD TO HURRY. He didn't like leaving Taylor alone for a minute. She was too pale, scared to death, and her attacker might still be on the premises. With ten thousand square feet of house and three acres, no telling where the bastard might be.

He could even be in the house. Had he tried to kill Taylor so he could rob her? Or could her brother, Miles, have attacked her because of her inheritance?

He yanked his boots back on, and they squeaked on the Italian marble tile as he entered the mansion. He paused to listen, but it was quiet. Too quiet. If the security system had been breached because of the power outage, it should be beeping. The security team would also have been notified and would have shown up by now.

Someone had disarmed the alarm intentionally.

He located the security system panel and pushed the manual button to open the gates, grateful to hear the sirens approaching. Then he jogged back outside to Taylor. He'd do a thorough search of the property, house and system once she was taken care of.

She was crouched in the lounge chair, clutching the towel around her, trembling. He scanned the area, walked to the edge of the gardens and checked. But he saw no movement in the carefully tailored layout of trimmed bushes and rose vines. Something caught his eye on a low tree branch. A hair had gotten caught in the twig. A long blond hair but not as blond as Taylor's. A woman's hair.

But Taylor said she'd been attacked by a man.

He bagged the hair anyway for trace.

On edge, he strode back to Taylor, this time standing guard. His jaw clenched at the sight of the scrapes and abrasions on her knees and hands. A bruise darkened her cheek and her nails were jagged and bloody, indicating she'd fought her assailant. Good for her.

Damn bastard. He couldn't stand the thought of any man beating on a woman. Maybe they'd find some trace evidence or DNA.

"What happened?" he asked bluntly.

She winced, biting down on her lip as if the horror of the memory was haunting her. "I came down for a swim," she whispered, coughing in between the words.

He grimaced, knowing her throat was hurting, her vocal chords damaged from the attack.

"He attacked you inside or out here?"

"Out here." She shuddered visibly. "I was swimming laps, then the lights went out." She paused, and her hand went involuntarily to her throat. Whether from pain or trauma he didn't know. Maybe both.

"Then I saw a movement beside the garden and got scared, so I swam to the edge and climbed out. I tried to make it inside, but he grabbed me from behind."

The siren screeched, announcing the arrival of the paramedics and Hayes leaned over Taylor. "I'll take you around front to them, then I'll search the premises."

She nodded although she tensed when he lifted her and raced to the ambulance. The EMTs met them, and two security officers screeched to a stop, also vaulting into motion. The CSI unit followed a second later.

A thin wiry security guard for Cantara Hills spoke first. "We have other teams dispatched, searching the surrounding houses, canvassing the neighborhood."

Hayes nodded while the EMTs examined Taylor. The CSI tech approached with a kit.

"Process her," he told them. Although the chlorinated water might have washed away or destroyed trace evidence.

"We'll need to take her in for X-rays, an EKG and lab work," one of the paramedics said.

Hayes angled his head toward Taylor. "I'll meet you at the hospital. I want to search the house first in case the perp is inside or left evidence."

Taylor's gaze sought his, and he offered a brusque smile. She looked incredibly small and fragile, as if she didn't want him to leave, but that was shock talking. She'd never given him the time of day before.

Shaking off the thought, he left her with the medics so he could focus on the crime scene.

One of the CSI agents began with Taylor while the second one followed him around to the terrace. "Consider the crime scene as the pool area and backyard," he told the criminologist. "Our victim first saw her attacker by the gardens, so check for footprints, trace, anything you can find."

He gestured around the terrace. "My guess is he knocked over that plant while trying to escape. He probably ran through the gardens, jumped the fence and disappeared on foot, so look for footprints. Maybe his car was parked on a neighboring street. Or maybe he lives nearby." Hell, by now he might have cleaned up, disposed of the clothes he'd worn during the attack and be safely in his house or bed.

Then again, Taylor hadn't been in the pool that long. Maybe he hadn't escaped.

Hopefully one of the security guys would turn up something. "I'm going to check the inside premises, see if our guy might be hiding in one of the rooms."

He hoped to hell he *was* inside Taylor's. Then he could arrest the SOB and make him pay for hurting her.

But first, he'd like to take a fist to him for the bruises on her face and neck.

And if he'd hired Montoya to kill Kimberly...

Well, if he had, Hayes had a good excuse to kill him.

TAYLOR COULDN'T SHAKE the realization that she'd almost died as she allowed the EMTs to examine her. If it hadn't been for Sergeant Hayes Keller, she would still be floating in that pool. Dead. Her life over.

And who would care?

Her opulent mansion with its thirty-plus rooms mocked her. She had Caroline, Margaret and Victoria, but no significant male....

The CSI technician, a young woman with sandy-blond hair, offered her a friendly smile. "We need to photograph your injuries, ma'am."

Taylor frowned, feeling violated all over again as she dropped the towel and the woman began to snap pictures.

While she tried to lift prints from Taylor's neck, then scraped beneath her fingernails, Taylor closed her eyes, focusing on anything besides the attack. But images of the Texas Ranger's eyes flickered in her head. She could still feel his breath on her face, his touch on her mouth. His dark eyes had held worry....

Impossible.

He didn't even like her. He was simply a cop doing a job.

But no man had ever treated her as gently as he had when he'd comforted her.

Good grief, she was pathetic. Was she so desperate for comfort that she'd conjure an attraction between them, and a heart in the cold man beneath that badge?

Her ping-ponging emotions must be due to her upcoming birthday. She was turning the big three-oh. Her biological clock was ticking like a time bomb. And although people assumed she'd host a big bash to celebrate, she wouldn't.

Besides, turning thirty had its own consequences. She'd inherit the millions from the trust fund her father had reserved for her.

Yet he wouldn't personally show to celebrate the big day.

And Miles, her half brother, would hate her even more.

The argument she'd had with him earlier taunted her. The resentment in his tone, the accusations in his eyes. For a moment, she'd been afraid of him. He'd gripped her arm and shouted at her, had sounded out of control, almost threatening. And then that phone call…

No. She didn't like the path her mind was taking.

Miles wouldn't try to kill her, would he?

Chapter Three

Hayes checked the circuit breakers and restored power before searching the mansion. Throwing some light in the house might drive out the perp, or at least strip the guy of his advantage.

He gripped his weapon in one hand and kept his eyes trained for the intruder as he moved through the lower level. Taylor's basement housed a fully equipped gym, rec room with pool table, bar and a movie theater, as well as a separate kitchen and two suites. Hell, her basement furnishings were nicer than anything he owned.

He slowly climbed the stairs, pausing to listen, but other than the hum of the air conditioner and the padding of his boots on the kitchen tiles as he eased through the breakfast room, the house was silent. He crossed the formal dining room, to the living room, to the office. Built-in bookshelves held a variety of titles, while the room held a state-of-the-art computer system, sitting area and conference table. Photographs of Taylor and her father, then Taylor at various charity functions, decorated the walls, along with award plaques and a framed diploma from a private school in Switzerland. She'd apparently earned a business degree and now ran the Landis Foundation.

So she was not only beautiful and rich but smart.

He stored that information while he checked the family room with fireplace and twelve-foot ceilings and a ballroom with Palladian windows which obviously was used to host her elaborate parties. He'd seen photographs of them in the society section of the newspaper.

A place where he wouldn't be caught dead.

Finally, he found his way through a hallway to a bedroom suite the size of an apartment.

He wondered if this was Taylor's suite, but saw no personal belongings in the room. Decorated in earth tones, it held a king-size brass bed, dresser, flat-screen TV and sitting room. A massive bath in gold and white with a Jacuzzi and dozens of plush towels overflowing a baker's rack opened to a large walk-in closet.

The suite was empty, so he headed back to the foyer, then climbed the curved staircase, again pausing to listen. But he heard nothing. He still couldn't relax, not until he'd searched every square inch of the house.

Taking a deep breath, he clenched his hand tighter around his gun and combed the suites to the left, then retraced his steps back to the bank of rooms on the right. In the first bedroom, a white four-poster bed draped in blue-and-white satin drew his eye.

Judging from the lived-in look and feminine furnishings, he guessed it was Taylor's room. A black satin robe lay draped across the bed and a pair of slippers peeked from beneath the footboard. The room looked like her—tasteful, classy, soft.

For a moment, he imagined her sprawled on the satin

sheets wearing nothing but a skimpy teddy or…nothing at all, and his body hardened with desire.

He quickly shook off the image. What in the hell was wrong with him?

An iPod and speaker system sat opposite the bed on a cluster of shelves holding candles, and in the corner a dresser held a silver brush and comb set and a jewelry box. He wondered if Taylor kept all her jewelry so accessible, but assumed she had a built-in safe somewhere in the house for her more expensive pieces. When she was released from the hospital, he'd have her check the house to see if anything was missing.

A bay window with chaise and reading lamp occupied one corner with a window seat separating two oversized chairs. He bypassed them and entered an elegant bath in blue and white, and a set of closets. Inside, he clenched his jaw at the sight of glittery gowns, expensive wraps, designer shoes and business suits. The second closet held Taylor's casual clothes, he assumed, since it was filled with sundresses, slacks, designer sweaters, and one wall housed shelves holding bathing suits and summer wear.

He snarled. His yearly salary wouldn't equal her monthly clothing allowance.

It didn't matter. He had to focus on his mission.

The rooms were empty, and didn't look as if they'd been touched by an intruder, meaning the perpetrator probably hadn't attacked her with the intention of theft.

So not a break-in gone awry. The perp's intentions had been more sinister—murder.

Moving on, he searched the other rooms, sighing as he descended the steps. Just as he was bypassing the office, he noticed a broken fingernail caught on the edge of the rug by the desk. He stooped and picked it up, wondering who it belonged to. The phone jangled so he bagged the fingernail, then hurried to the desk and checked the caller ID. An international call. Her father?

He picked up the receiver. "Taylor Landis's residence."

A long moment of silence. "Who in the hell is this?"

"Sergeant Hayes Keller, Texas Ranger. Whom am I speaking with?"

"Lionel Landis. What's going on? Why are you at my daughter's house? And why are you answering her phone?"

Hayes grimaced at the man's condescending tone. But he had a right to know his daughter had been attacked. And Hayes had to explore every angle. If the assault on Taylor wasn't related to Kimberly's murder, it might have something to do with the wealthy Landis family. Then he'd need information on the family and their business dealings.

"Sir, I hate to have to tell you this, but your daughter was assaulted tonight."

"What? My God, is she all right?"

"Yes, sir. But the paramedics transported her to the hospital for X-rays and observation."

"I heard about those break-ins in the community. Was that what this was about?"

"I don't know yet, but I can assure you I'll find out."

A long pause. "Maybe I should hire a bodyguard to watch her around the clock."

Hayes clenched his jaw. Odd that her father didn't offer to fly back to see her himself. Instead, he wanted to send hired help.

A private bodyguard would mean Hayes wouldn't have to spend time with Taylor himself.

But damn. He was a ranger, and he had to finish this case, find the man who'd tried to kill Taylor. "That won't be necessary, Mr. Landis. I'll personally provide protection for your daughter 24-7."

He hung up the phone but noticed the desk drawer ajar and examined it. The bottom drawer had been jimmied, papers tossed around.

The killer had been in this room. He'd have CSI dust it for prints.

What had he been looking for?

EXHAUSTION WEIGHED ON TAYLOR as the nurse helped her settle into the hospital bed. She'd been treated, had blood drawn, undergone an EKG, then wheeled to X-ray where they'd x-rayed her chest and lungs. Thankfully all the tests were clear.

Other than nearly dying tonight, she was healthy.

Still, they'd hooked her up to an IV, checked her vitals, then the nurse offered her a sedative. But Taylor expected Sergeant Keller to show up any minute to question her, and she wanted to be coherent.

Besides, she avoided taking pills or medications unless it was absolutely necessary. Too many people she'd met at parties relied on drugs or alcohol for recreation and survival, and she was determined not to fall into that dangerous lifestyle so often portrayed in the tabloids as the rich and careless.

Still, fatigue pulled at her, and she finally dozed off. But nightmares of the attack haunted her, and she tossed and turned, battling the terrifying memories.

She was running, fighting, struggling for air, being pushed under the water, held down…drowning.

She woke, gasping for air, her heart racing. Gray had settled over the room like a fog, the sound of someone breathing echoing in the quiet. Panic shot through her.

Oh, God, her attacker had come here to finish killing her.

She threw off the covers to run, but suddenly two firm hands gripped her arms. "Shh, Taylor, it's me. Hayes."

She was just about to scream, but the sound of his husky voice registered, and she stifled a sob.

"I didn't mean to scare you, but you were sleeping."

She relaxed against him, but her heart was still pounding. "I was dreaming about the attack…."

He smoothed her hair from her cheek, then eased down onto the edge of the bed. "It's over now. You're safe."

She nodded and forced herself to block out the terrifying images from her nightmare. Despite her efforts, her hand went to her throat.

"You didn't find him at the house?" she asked.

He shook his head, and she noticed he was wearing the same jeans and shirt he had on when he'd pulled her from the pool. They were still damp, and he must be uncomfortable, but he didn't seem to notice.

"Your assailant caused the power outage by tampering with the circuit breakers, but I didn't find anyone inside. CSI is dusting for prints and searching both the inside and outside, as well, for footprints, fibers, anything that might help us identify him."

"He didn't steal anything?"

"Not that I could tell. But you'll need to inventory your valuables, jewelry, etcetera; to verify if anything is missing."

"I'll do that tomorrow when I get home."

He gave a clipped nod. "The desk in your office had been ransacked. Do you have any idea what the intruder might have been looking for?"

She shook her head. "Maybe financial information on the foundation?"

"It's possible. You should examine your files and follow up on any credit cards."

She bit her lip. "Yes, I will."

"I left a guard at the house overnight in case he returns or someone else shows up."

"Thank you, Sergeant."

"You can call me Hayes." He hesitated, then his gaze zeroed in on her nails. "Your nails are real?"

She nodded. "Why?"

"I found a broken red nail, looked like an acrylic, inside your house."

She frowned. "I often have guests over, females. It could have come from any one of them."

"You're sure your attacker was male?"

His question threw her off guard. "I think so."

"I also found a blond hair caught in a twig in the tree by the garden."

She rubbed her temple. "I have parties out there, too. It could belong to anyone."

"I'll see what forensics says." He paused. "Can you talk about the attack now?"

She propped herself up against the pillows. "I told you what happened already."

"Indulge me and go over it again. Sometimes the passage of time allows victims to remember more details."

She sighed, hating to rehash the night but knowing it was imperative. "Okay. I got home around ten, but I was restless, antsy after all that's happened in the neighborhood lately." In fact, she hadn't slept well since Kimberly McQuade had died. If she hadn't hosted the party that night, maybe the young woman would still be alive.

She glanced at Hayes, suddenly realizing that he probably felt the same way, probably blamed her.

"Go on," he said sharply.

She cleared her throat; it was still so dry it hurt to talk. "I couldn't sleep, so I checked the alarm and changed into my swimsuit. Then I went for a swim."

"Had you been drinking?"

Irritation gnawed at her. "I had a glass of wine with dinner, but I wasn't drunk if that's what you're implying."

"You usually swim alone at night?"

She tensed at the scrutiny in his tone. Did he think she was being stupid, that she'd brought the attack on herself? "Sometimes," she said truthfully. "I'm a good swimmer, and I had the security system set." She glared at him. "Besides, I thought you rangers had caught the killer and that I was safe."

A muscle ticked in his jaw, and she knew she'd scored a direct hit.

"Your attack may or may not be related to the other crimes," he said sharply. "You're wealthy, everyone knows that. You must have some enemies."

She tore her gaze away with a shiver. If he'd meant to scare her, he had.

"Were the lights on when you came out by the pool?"

"Yes, Sergeant. I would have called security if they hadn't been."

He simply arched a dark brow, his expression cold and hard, and she silently willed herself to stop reacting. What did she care what Hayes Keller thought of her?

When she continued, she tried to relay the events as if it had happened to a stranger, not to her. "I was swimming laps when the power flickered off. I got nervous, decided to see what caused the outage, then I saw a movement by the gardens. I got out and ran toward the door… Before I reached it, the man jumped me from behind." She paused, unable to breathe for a moment as she remembered his fingers around her throat.

Again, the ranger stared at her with an intensity that made her more nervous.

She could not break down in front of the man again. "We struggled and he tried to strangle me, then we fell into the pool."

"He fell into the pool with you?"

"Yes. I fought him, but he kept choking me, then pushed me underwater and held me down."

He made a low sound with his teeth. "That's probably the reason he turned on the water hose, to wash away his prints. But I'll have the pool dragged for trace." He paused. "You said you were a swimmer?"

"Yes, high-school swim team. I set the record for holding my breath the longest on my team."

"That's probably what saved you."

"No, Sergeant Keller, you saved me," she said with a

tentative smile. "If you hadn't shown up when you had…"

He glanced away for the first time, his jaw clenched tight, then shrugged. "Just doing my job, ma'am."

She didn't like the way he said *ma'am*, as if it was an insult. "Well, thank you anyway."

His eyes darkened, narrowed to slits as if he was issuing some kind of silent warning. "You don't owe me thanks. Just answer the questions."

She tensed at his brusque tone. Just when she thought he was human, he turned back into a growling lion. "What else do you want to know?"

The bite to her voice echoed in the silence for a moment before he replied. "You didn't see the man's face?"

"No. He was wearing a mask."

"Like a ski mask?"

"Yes. And gloves. Latex gloves."

His brows pinched together with his frown. "Maybe those will turn up or we'll lift some trace off of your fingernails."

She nodded, glad she'd fought back.

"Anything else you remember about your attacker? A particular odor? His height, size?"

"No, it's all so foggy."

His dark gaze met hers. "Tell me about your day, what happened earlier, before the attack."

She scrunched her nose in thought. "I don't see how that's relevant."

"Just do it, Taylor. Retrace your steps."

"All right, but you don't have to be so ornery." She tried to think back. "I spent the morning handling routine business matters for the foundation. Had lunch there. Then a business meeting with the City Board at five that ran till about seven. After that, I met a friend for dinner in San Antonio."

"Did you notice anyone following you during the day? Or when you left the restaurant?"

She rubbed her temple where a headache pulsed. "No."

He folded his arms. "Who attended the board meeting?"

"All of the board members. Sarah DeMarco, Devon Goldenrod—"

"Kenneth Sutton?"

"Yes."

"I was told that he and Kimberly McQuade had an argument before she died. Do you know what their disagreement was about?"

She frowned. "No. Kimberly was looking over the campaign budget, and she'd also reviewed the other finances for the board. Maybe there was a problem."

"So they might have argued about money?"

"I really don't know. Why is that important?"

"I'm just tying up loose ends. Sometimes small details can offer clues."

She conceded his point. After all, he was the cop. The chip-on-the-shoulder one, but it looked as if she was stuck with him.

"So, did anything unusual happen at the meeting?"

She hesitated, hated to impugn Kenneth unnecessarily.

"Taylor, I can't help you if you don't tell me the truth."

"Kenneth seemed excited about planning ahead for the gubernatorial election, but we did have a tense moment."

He leaned forward. "About what?"

"The bid for the new city library and to extend the

tourist area by the Riverwalk. There's talk that the bid was tampered with."

"And that Kenneth was involved?"

"That's what I've heard, but he denied it and I believe him."

Silence met her statement, making her wonder what he was thinking. "You don't like Kenneth Sutton, do you?"

"He's a politician. No, I don't trust him.

"And after the meeting? Who did you have dinner with?"

She hesitated.

"Taylor?"

She twisted her hands together. "Margaret Hathaway."

His jaw tightened again. "You two are friends?"

"Yes. We met at our favorite restaurant and sushi bar, Bluefish. Margaret's wedding to Devon Goldenrod is around the corner, and we were finalizing wedding plans."

"Did anything unusual happen while you were there?"

"Not unusual. But I ran into my half brother, Miles."

His mouth thinned. "How did that go?"

She sighed, knotting the bedsheet between her fingers. She hated to discuss family. But if the ranger asked at the restaurant, he'd find out on his own. Her problems with her brother weren't exactly a secret.

"Taylor, I know that Miles has been hitting up friends for loans. Caroline told us that already." He cleared his throat. "Is that what he wanted with you?"

So much for family privacy. Then again, she should be used to it. Just because she was wealthy, tabloids, reporters and neighbors thought her life was food for the gossipmongers. "Yes, but I turned him down again. He blew up, made a scene…."

She looked away, his phone call echoing in her head.

Hayes narrowed his eyes. "He threatened you, didn't he?"

She sucked in a sharp breath. "Not exactly."

"What does that mean?"

She finally faced him. "He told me I'd be sorry for turning my back on him."

He stood, bracing his feet apart, and hooked his thumbs in his belt loops. "That sounds like a threat to me."

She shrugged, unable to voice the truth. That she was afraid of Miles.

"I've posted a guard outside your door."

"You think that's necessary?"

He nodded. "And your father called your house. I told him I'd protect you 24-7."

Taylor's stomach dipped.

"I'm going to talk to your little brother. Find out if he tried to make good on his threat." His snakeskin cowboy boots pounded the floor as he pivoted. "Meanwhile, think hard, Taylor. In the morning I want you to make a list of any enemies you might have, former boyfriends or current ones who might want to harm you. Is there one you can think of offhand?"

She lowered her head. "No. I haven't been involved with anyone recently."

"In the past?"

She hadn't broken any hearts if that's what he meant. She'd never let a man get that close. "Maybe this was a random break-in."

"Just make the list. If it wasn't a robbery then someone wanted you dead."

A chill went through her. "You don't have to remind me, Sergeant."

"No? Well, think about this. The person who tried to strangle you could be someone you know from the foundation, someone who has it in for your family, someone who wants your money."

His dark gaze pierced her. "And it very well may be someone you know and trust, someone you're even close to. Someone you think is a friend, or your very own brother."

Chapter Four

Taylor's heart raced. Surely the ranger was wrong. None of her friends would actually harm her. Although neither she nor Caroline had thought that Carlson Woodward was dangerous and they'd been mistaken.

And what about Miles? He'd always been jealous of her and had done some underhanded things when they were younger, but he'd never been violent.

Not until recently. But lately she'd seen a spark flare in his eyes that scared her.

His substance abuse and gambling problems had escalated, making him seem desperate at times, and…frightening.

A knock sounded at the door, and suddenly Margaret Hathaway rushed in, her face stricken with concern.

"Oh my God, Taylor, I heard what happened. Are you all right?"

Taylor clenched the sheets as Hayes gave Margaret a feral look, a look that nearly froze Margaret in her rush to hug Taylor.

"I'm fine, Margaret," Taylor said, although tears

blurred her sight. She could hold herself together in the face of Hayes's brusqueness, but her best friend's tenderness unraveled her calm facade. Although Margaret was old enough to be her mother, they had bonded as soon as they had met. The one person in the world Taylor trusted, the one who loved her unconditionally, was Margaret. And Taylor felt the same way about her friend. Not only was Margaret smart but kindhearted, and she'd faced her own share of problems and pain, although she hid them well from the prying eyes of the public.

Margaret bypassed Hayes and swept Taylor into a hug. "God, this is awful, Tay. What happened?"

Taylor relayed the short version of the story, well aware of Hayes's scowl.

"Who in the world would want to hurt you, honey?"

"I don't know, Margaret." Taylor sighed. "But Sergeant Keller saved my life."

Surprise registered on Margaret's face, then she gave Hayes a curious look and smiled. "Sergeant, thank you so much for rescuing Taylor. I don't know what I'd do if anything happened to her."

Hayes's dark eyes turned icy. "Just doing my job, ma'am. Where were you this evening?"

"Sergeant Keller, you're out of line," Taylor said sharply.

"Like I told you earlier, Miss Landis, your attacker could be one of your friends."

"It certainly isn't Margaret," Taylor said between clenched teeth. "She would never hurt me."

"That's right," Margaret said, obviously insulted at the thought. "Taylor and I are best friends."

"Then you won't mind answering my question," Hayes said in a lethal voice.

Margaret tightened her jaw, and Taylor gripped her hand. "I told you she wouldn't hurt me."

"I had dinner with Taylor, then met my fiancé, Devon Goldenrod, at his house," Margaret said. "You can ask him."

Hayes arched a brow. "Right, the golden boy who's vying for votes in the next City Board election."

Taylor grimaced at the disdain in Hayes's voice. She'd heard he'd had a rough life but he didn't have to take his attitude out on her and Margaret.

Then again, for a moment, pain had flashed in his eyes when he'd seen Margaret hug her. Kimberly had mentioned that he'd been adopted, that there were some things he refused to talk about.

Margaret folded her arms. "Sergeant, what are you doing to find the person who attacked Taylor?"

His lips thinned into a deeper frown. "I've processed the crime scene and will be investigating everyone in Miss Landis's life for motive."

"What about keeping her safe?" Margaret asked.

An evil grin slid across the ranger's face. "Well, ma'am," he drawled mockingly, "I've got that covered."

"How?" Margaret asked.

"I've been assigned as her bodyguard day and night."

Taylor's stomach sizzled with nerves yet she pressed her fingers to her lips, remembering how gentle he'd been when he resuscitated her. How in the world was she going to endure being near this man when he obviously hated everything about her?

HAYES BALLED HIS HANDS into fists to control his temper. Dammit, Taylor Landis looked all soft and needy. And she'd touched those luscious lips and looked up at him as if she was remembering his mouth on hers when he'd brought her back to life.

Hell. He couldn't think about that. Couldn't touch her mouth or any other part of her body again.

So he lashed out at her by taking perverse joy in taunting her rich friend. Maybe it was payback for all the taunting he'd received as a kid.

Margaret narrowed her eyes. "For some reason that doesn't make me feel any better, Sergeant."

He threw his head back and chuckled. "Don't worry, Ms. Hathaway, I won't let anything bad happen to the little princess."

"You'd better not." Margaret's eyes flashed with emotions that Hayes refused to allow to get to him. "Because she's going to be my maid of honor at my wedding, and I don't want her showing up in a cast or on crutches."

Or not showing up because she was dead, Hayes thought, although he refrained from comment. "In light of the fact that someone tried to kill you tonight, Taylor, you shouldn't put yourself in the limelight right now."

Margaret's face blanched with fear, and Hayes's gut tightened.

"He's right," Margaret said. "I'll postpone everything until after the police find out who did this to you, Tay."

"No, you won't," Taylor said, shooting Hayes a harsh look.

"But I don't want to take a chance on you being hurt," Margaret argued.

"She's right, Taylor," Hayes said. "You need to go into hiding until we find the man who attacked you."

Anger sizzled in Taylor's sky-blue eyes. "I refuse to run and hide. I'm not going to let some creep scare me from living my life."

Hayes glared at her. "Then you're a fool and asking for trouble."

She turned a saccharine sweet smile on Hayes that was so fake it fueled his temper. "But, Sergeant, you'll be with me day and night to protect me."

He met her gaze with a sinister stare, but she smiled again, and focused on Margaret as if he was her minion.

Rage ripped through him. That was how she saw him, and he couldn't forget it.

AS SOON AS MARGARET LEFT, Taylor fell into an exhausted sleep. Fitful images of the attack drove her awake several times, but when she opened her eyes, she saw Hayes Keller sitting in the chair in the corner watching her. She shouldn't have found comfort in having him close by, but his big masculine presence soothed her nerves, and she rolled to her side and drifted back to sleep.

The last time she woke, sunlight streamed through the hospital window, and she checked the chair. He was slightly slumped, his head having fallen sideways in sleep, and his massive chest moved up and down with his breath. Catching him off guard in sleep seemed somehow *intimate*.

She noticed the fine dark stubble along his rugged jaw, the way his thick lips formed a constant scowl, the little curl in his dark hair that made her want to run her hands through it. His jaw was broad, his nose blunt and slightly crooked as if it had been broken and his eyebrows were full and thick, arched to frame his eyes in a way that added to his intensity.

The sound of his breathing floated toward her, a coarse whisper just as masculine as his face and body.

Somehow in that moment, he looked almost... human. And approachable.

He suddenly opened his eyes, his gaze meeting hers, and a tingling started low and deep in her belly. Lord, he was potently sexy. Like a cowboy hero in a Western.

No, no, no. She couldn't allow herself to fantasize about him.

His eyebrows lifted slightly, and a heartbeat of silence stretched between them, fraught with tension.

She must be insane because at that moment she wanted him.

Then the door swung open and the doctor walked in. "Good morning, Miss Landis. Let's see if it's time to dismiss you."

Hayes pushed to his feet, his boots pounding as he walked to the door. "I'll be outside. Let me know when you're ready to leave."

She nodded, although her throat was too thick to speak. She could count on her hand the number of men she'd actually been this attracted to over the years.

Why did Hayes Keller have to be one of them?

HAYES PACED OUTSIDE TAYLOR'S hospital room. What in the hell had just happened?

After endless hours of being tortured by watching Taylor toss and turn, of wanting to crawl in bed and comfort her when she'd cried out in terror from her nightmares, he'd finally dozed off, only to have his own demons haunt him.

He had been five years old, locked in that damn closet where his adopted parents stuffed him anytime they needed to go out. Or when they just needed some peace and quiet.

Or when they wanted to punish him for being bad. And according to them, he was bad all the time so he'd spent half his young life in that tiny dark closet.

He still had claustrophobia. Hated dark closets, basements and crawl spaces.

Hell, he was a grown man now. Had his own life. A nice little cabin he'd built himself on a small ranch with tons of light where no one could bother him, where he'd never be stuck in that dark place again.

And he wouldn't…not even in his mind.

He had escaped and had a job to do, and he'd damn well do it without allowing Taylor to get under his skin like she had earlier.

He'd survived that hellhole of a family. He could survive being assigned as her bodyguard.

All the more reason to find her attacker quickly, though, so he could leave Cantara Hills.

The door opened and the doctor appeared, Taylor's chart in hand. "She's dressing, then she can go home."

He nodded. Margaret had brought Taylor an overnight bag. A nurse appeared with a wheelchair, and he went and retrieved his SUV from the parking garage, then pulled up in front of the hospital. Taylor climbed in and fastened her seat belt, and he maneuvered into the early morning traffic and drove to Cantara Hills.

"If we're forced to spend time together, we should get to know each other," Taylor said, filling the awkward silence.

He glared at her. "I intend to learn everything about you."

Her blond brows rose, eyes sparkling. "Really?"

He pressed his mouth into a frown. "Yes, and all your friends."

The light left her eyes. "Then tell me about yourself. About your family."

A muscle ticked in his jaw. "I'm here to do a job, Taylor. My personal life is off-limits."

For a brief second, hurt tugged at her expression.

He turned away from her, refused to feel guilty. "I need to go by my room at the country club and pick up my duffel bag."

"Excuse me?" she said quietly.

"I told you I'm your bodyguard. That means I'm moving in."

She shivered and hugged her arms around her waist. "I certainly hope you find whoever did this quickly."

He chuckled. She obviously didn't want him around any more than he wanted to be with her. "That's the plan. In fact, I'd like to clean up and then I want to talk to your brother and Kenneth Sutton."

She stared out the window, her expression pained. "I just can't believe one of them would try to kill me."

He clamped his mouth shut. She was too damn innocent. Just because these people were related to her or acted as if they were her friends, didn't mean they didn't have secrets or a motive for murder.

Chapter Five

Taylor grimaced at the way Hayes had cut her off when she'd inquired about his family. She felt for him, but she couldn't continue offering friendship if he was going to be so rude.

Besides, as soon as he found out who'd tried to kill her, he'd ride out of Cantara Hills and never look back.

She'd had it with men either using her or disappearing when they'd finished their agenda.

He parked in the circular drive, and she jumped out, not bothering to wait for him to open the door for her. The inside of the car had been too crowded, too hot, too filled with his male scent.

So why did his eyes haunt her?

Frustration mingled with fear as she unlocked the door. But Hayes pushed her aside and ordered her to wait while he checked the house. She paced nervously. She'd always felt safe here, but after the night before, would she ever feel safe again?

At least her estate was large so she and Hayes wouldn't be trapped in close quarters together. She noticed her office door ajar and veered inside to see if anything was missing. Thankfully, she kept her important papers, stocks and bonds, in a safe, and she examined it first, then breathed a sigh of relief. Next she searched the desk files, but didn't notice anything missing. Even the file she'd been reviewing regarding the discrepancy with the city council bids seemed intact.

What had the intruder been looking for? What had been important enough for him to have killed her to get it?

HAYES NOTICED THE STRICKEN look on Taylor's face. The reality of her home invasion had finally hit her. But he steeled himself against sympathy. "Did you notice anything missing?"

She shook her head, then tucked a strand of her long blond hair behind one ear. "The safe hasn't been open, and all my files are intact."

So what had the killer been looking for?

"Inventory your jewelry."

She nodded and he followed her to her suite. She looked wary as she entered her bedroom, and he remained at the threshold, shifting to lean against the frame while she sorted through her jewelry. The sight of diamonds and the glittering emeralds and sapphires served as a reminder of the yawning distance between them.

"Is everything there?"

She bit down on her bottom lip. "Yes…wait. Let me look at my other jewelry box."

She had two?

He tugged at his Stetson as she opened her closet and retrieved a smaller box from the top shelf. The box was intricately carved, black lacquered, an Asian design although small, almost as if it had belonged to a child. She traced a finger over it lovingly and he wondered if it held special meaning for her. Maybe a gift from Daddy or a former lover?

The thought sent a small pang of jealousy streaking through him, but he brushed it off. What did he care if she had a dozen lovers? He would never be one of them.

"Taylor?"

She inhaled sharply, then lifted the lid, and her chin quivered. "It's gone."

"What?"

"My charm bracelet," she said softly.

"What was it worth?"

She lifted her head, and emotions splintered her eyes. "Not much, but it was priceless to me. My mother gave it to me." Her voice broke. "She used to add a charm every year at Christmas."

And her mother had died when she was eight.

"Why would someone take that piece instead of all those jewels in your other chest?" he asked.

"I don't know," she said, although the odd catch in her voice told him she was lying. "It's not valuable, not monetarily, I mean. But it was special to me."

He cleared his throat. "It had to be someone who knew where you kept it." Meaning the thief had meant to hurt her because he knew she valued the piece. "You think your brother stole it?"

She hesitated so long he had his answer. "Let me clean up and I'll pay Miles a visit," she said.

"I'm going with you, but I'd like to shower first."

He wanted to question Miles without her, yet he couldn't leave her alone, not knowing she was in danger, so he agreed, then headed downstairs to the guest suite.

But as he stripped and climbed in beneath the warm water, he imagined her upstairs doing the same. They could have conserved water if they'd showered together.

A bitter laugh lodged in his throat. Hell, he had to be honest, at least to himself. He didn't care about conserving water.

He was a hot-blooded man. He just wanted to see the damn woman naked.

TAYLOR STEWED OVER the bracelet while she showered. She didn't want to believe her brother would take the charm bracelet, because he understood its significance to her.

Yet he had been furious with her the last time they'd run in to each other.

She dressed in a pair of her favorite jeans and a sleeveless silk tank and hurried down the stairs. Hayes stood in the foyer in a crisp white shirt and jeans, his Stetson shadowing his face.

"Do you know where to find Miles?"

She glanced at the grandfather clock. "At this time of the morning, he'll still be sleeping off last night's party."

"Then let's go wake him up," Hayes said.

Her stomach quivered as they walked to his SUV, and she studied the landscape architecture of the community as he drove to Miles's house, an English Tudor her father had bought for him for his twenty-first birthday. Of course, Miles had pouted that it wasn't as large as the estate where Taylor lived, which had only increased the tension between the two of them.

But she actually earned a salary, and kept the mansion to host various charity functions for the foundation. She took pride in using her salary for her own personal causes—she and Margaret funded a special program for needy children and Margaret spearheaded one for pregnant teens.

"This is it?" Hayes asked as he parked in front of the Tudor.

"Yes."

"He lives alone?"

"Most of the time, but he entertains a lot. Mostly women."

"Your brother is the party guy, isn't he?"

"I'm afraid so." To the detriment of himself and anyone who cared about him.

They climbed out, and she led the way to her brother's front door. Hayes punched the doorbell, tapping his boot on the brick stoop as they waited. Impatience made Taylor stab the button again.

No answer, so she retrieved her keys from her purse and unlocked the door. "He has to be here. It's too early for him to be out for the day."

"Maybe he spent the night with his latest hook-up."

"That's possible," Taylor said as she pushed her way inside.

"Does Miles have a key to your house?" Hayes asked.

Her gaze swung to his, and she released a sigh. "Yes."

He shook his head in disgust, and she bolted up the stairs toward his room. "Miles, it's me, Taylor. Are you up there?"

No answer.

"Miles, I hope you're decent, because I'm coming in."

She pounded on his door, and Hayes stood behind her, his presence oddly comforting as she opened it. "Miles?"

A low growl erupted, and she spotted him in bed, the covers half over him, a bottle of Scotch on the nightstand.

She stormed through the room, grabbed the slacks he'd tossed on the floor and threw them at him. "Get dressed. We have to talk."

"What in the hell are you doing here?" He scrubbed a hand through his scraggly hair and glanced at the clock. "Good God, Taylor. It's only ten o'clock in the morning."

"At ten o'clock, most people have already been at work for two hours," she snapped.

"Get out of here!" he shouted, then rolled over and pulled the comforter over his head.

Hayes jerked the covers from his face. "Either dress and join us downstairs or I'll drag you there myself."

Taylor smiled. If anyone could coerce the truth from her brother, it would be Hayes Keller.

HAYES IGNORED MILES'S LITANY of profanities as he stepped outside the man's room. He, Egan and Brody had already speculated about Miles's motive. The twenty-four-year-old could have taken advantage of Kimberly's death to kill Taylor by pretending to be a vigilante killer, murdering suspects and witnesses involved in Kimberly's death to cover up his real target—his sister. All so he could gain access to Taylor's inheritance.

Taylor walked ahead down the staircase, her irritation with her brother evident by the strain on her face.

He followed her to the kitchen where she brewed coffee. By the time Miles stumbled into the room, she'd poured both herself and Hayes a cup, then handed a third mug to her brother. He reeked of booze and cigarettes and a sour attitude.

"All right, Taylor. What is such a big freaking deal you came over here? And why is this ranger with you? You shacking up with him or something?"

Hayes knotted his hands, barely resisting the urge to ram his fist in the idiot's mouth. He'd put up with spoiled rich kids like him all his life, treating him like a third-class citizen.

Taylor's blue eyes glimmered with emotions. "Did you take the charm bracelet Mother gave me?"

Anger stained Miles's already flushed cheeks. "You dragged me out of bed because of that stupid trinket?"

"It's not stupid, Miles," Taylor said. "That was the only personal thing I have from Mom, and you know how much it meant to me."

He narrowed his eyes. "Yeah, but it's not worth anything, so why would I take it?"

"I don't know." Taylor's voice warbled with emotions. "Maybe you wanted to hurt me for not loaning you money."

Miles pushed his face into Taylor's like some childhood bully. "If I wanted to get back at you, I wouldn't pussyfoot around with some dinky bracelet. I'd go for something worth my time."

And money, Hayes thought grimly. Miles's daddy had probably bailed him out of trouble all his life, but if Hayes discovered he'd attacked Taylor, Hayes would make certain the guy paid.

He jerked Miles by the collar of his polo shirt. "So what would you do?" Hayes asked. "Try to kill her?"

Miles wheeled around on him. "Kill her? What in the hell are you talking about?"

"Where were you last night?" Hayes asked in a barely controlled tone.

Miles's eyes widened in alarm as he realized the implication. "Why do you want to know?"

Taylor crossed her arms over her chest. "Answer him, Miles."

Miles glanced back and forth between the two of them, fear and hate emanating from him. "I went clubbing. Took a cab home this morning."

"Can anyone vouch for you?" Hayes asked.

Though the earring in his left ear glinted in the sunlight, his face paled slightly. "I don't know, the bars were crowded."

"So you don't have an alibi?"

Temper flared in Miles's bloodshot eyes. "Do I need one?"

"Yes. Someone tried to kill your sister," Hayes said. "And you have a motive."

Miles backed up as if he thought Hayes might physically attack him. "Listen, I got drunk, went dancing. There's no way you're going to pin anything on me." He reached for the phone. "I'll call my attorney."

The weasel had shown no concern for Taylor at all. "You mean, you'll call your daddy to come to the rescue?" Hayes said snidely.

Miles's nostrils flared. "Guys like you have a chip

on their shoulder," Miles muttered. "Everyone in Cantara Hills has talked about it. You'd try to railroad me because you're jealous of my money."

Rage burned Hayes's throat. "I'm not jealous of anything *you* have."

Miles jerked an accusatory look toward Taylor. "He is, isn't he, Taylor? He knows he's not good enough for the women here, so he's trying to make you doubt your own family."

Hayes's temper snapped. This time he jammed his face into Miles's, intentionally proving he was bigger and stronger. "If I discover you tried to hurt your sister, I'll come after you so fast you won't know what hit you. And no amount of Daddy's money will save you."

Deciding he had to leave before he pelted the little weasel, he stalked toward the door. He heard Taylor's footfalls as she hurried along behind him, but he didn't look back. Didn't want her to know how deeply her pissant brother's comment had cut him.

Chapter Six

Taylor almost laughed at the sheer look of terror on Miles's face.

Was he afraid of Hayes because he really believed the ranger was out to nail him or because he had something to hide?

"What do you think?" Hayes asked her as they settled in his car.

"I don't know," she said, scrunching her face in worry. "Over the years Miles and I have had our differences, but he is still my half brother."

"One who's jealous as hell of you," Hayes said. "And he has a substance-abuse problem, owes heavy debts and may be desperate."

All true. Still, the thought of one of her own family members trying to take her life made bile rise in her throat. "Families are supposed to love and trust each other," she said quietly. "They should stick together, support each other in difficult times."

"It doesn't always work like that," Hayes commented dryly.

Still, sadness weighed on her. When her mother had

died, her father had thrown himself into work and travel, then sifted through women and marriages as easily as she did shoes. She'd needed him around, yet he'd chosen work and other women over raising his daughter. Then there had been the long line of nannies. And Miles had come along…

At first she'd been excited about having a little brother, but as he'd grown up, things had changed.

Miles had resented any attention their father had given her. One memory surfaced, a time when he'd cut off all of her dolls' hair, then blamed her. And another when he'd smashed the music box their father had given her.

Suddenly she felt a hand cover hers. When she looked up, Hayes was watching her, compassion in his eyes. He understood what it was like to be hurt by family.

"Let's talk to Kenneth Sutton now. He was upset with Kimberly for questioning him on the bids. And you asked him about it, too, didn't you?"

She nodded. "But I've worked with Kenneth for some time now, Hayes. I respect his ethics and his view on politics. I can't imagine him doing anything underhanded."

"He's a politician," Hayes said. "Maybe he thought no one would find out. With his campaign run for governor, it's even more important that anything illicit he was involved in be kept a secret."

She grimaced, praying Hayes was wrong and that she hadn't been fooled by Kenneth.

HAYES HADN'T MEANT TO TAKE Taylor's hand, but she'd seemed so fragile and sad that he hadn't been able to resist. She'd been through an ordeal the past twenty-four hours and had shown amazing strength.

Even rich little girls had problems, he admitted silently. Even rich families could be dysfunctional.

Still, he kept his opinion to himself. He was here to do a job, not coddle Taylor. Miles's comment only further reminded him that their worlds might coexist but didn't mix.

"Taylor, do you mind calling Sutton to make sure he's at his office before we drop by?"

"Sure." She retrieved her cell phone from her purse and punched in the number. He started the engine but waited while she asked Sutton's secretary if he was in.

"Thanks, Dora, tell Kenneth that Ranger Keller and I will be right there."

She hung up, then he maneuvered into traffic. A strained silence stretched between them, the heat in the car climbing to an uncomfortable level.

"What made you decide to become a Texas Ranger?" Taylor finally asked.

He frowned, squinting through the bright sun glinting off the front window, and flipped the air conditioner up a notch. "I guess Brody paved the path. When he joined, he talked about the training and chasing down the bad guys..." He shrugged. "Figured it was better than being one of them, and I was headed down that path."

He'd had a lot of anger built up from the Kellers and would never have survived if he hadn't made friends with Egan, Kimberly and Brody.

"Kimberly told me you guys were all friends as kids."

"Yeah, we grew up in the same neighborhood, although our backgrounds were different."

"You don't have to come from the same background to get along," Taylor murmured.

He jerked his head sideways. "They weren't the same but they weren't that different." Not like the two of them.

"Kimberly said your foster parents weren't very nice."

He scrubbed a hand over the back of his neck and felt it sweating. "Kim talked too much."

"She cared about you," Taylor said softly.

A pang squeezed his chest, reminding him of her death and the events that had brought them to Cantara Hills. He couldn't discuss Kimberly with Taylor. Kimberly had understood where he'd come from, what it was like to be thrown away by a parent. What it had been like to want something that you'd never had.

Taylor had lived a charmed life and understood none of that. She might be drawn to him now but only because of the danger and the close quarters. Or maybe she saw him as a new kind of adventure in her life. Maybe she'd wanted to see what it was like to slum.

So he clammed up, intentionally killing any more personal conversation between them.

Thankfully, they arrived at Sutton's office, and Hayes parked. As soon as they entered, Hayes smelled the scent of old money, politics and secrets.

Mountains of posters advertising Sutton as the candidate to vote for in the upcoming gubernatorial election were stacked in every conceivable space and a flurry of workers were stationed in a bullpen answering phones, accepting donations and fielding questions.

Sutton's secretary buzzed them in immediately.

Dressed in a designer suit with polished shoes that shone as brightly as his pearly whites, Sutton gestured for them to enter. "It's a madhouse around here, but please sit down. Would you like coffee?"

"No, thanks," Hayes said. "We're here on business."

Sutton's neatly trimmed hair looked spiked with gel, his eyebrows waxed, his nails manicured, his forehead furrowed. "If it's about those bids, I have my people looking into that. I'm sure it's some kind of clerical error. That or someone is trying to sabotage my campaign by slandering my name and reputation."

"The bids are the least of your worries right now," Hayes said. "Where were you last night?"

Tension rippled between them, and Hayes saw the wheels turning in Sutton's eyes. Should he phone his lawyer?

Sutton glanced at Taylor. "What's this about, Taylor?"

Hayes ground his teeth. Sutton was smooth, intentionally using his personal connection to Taylor to his advantage. Just how personal was it?

Egan mentioned that Sutton's wife, Tammy, might be sleeping around, but what about Kenneth?

"Kenneth, I'm sorry," Taylor began.

"Last night someone tried to kill Taylor," Hayes said bluntly.

"Good God almighty." Sutton lurched from his chair and circled around to study Taylor. "What happened? Are you okay?"

"Answer my question first." Hayes cut in. "Where were you last night?"

Anger flashed in Sutton's eyes for a brief second, but he recovered quickly and pasted on his politician's smile. The man had appeared to be genuinely concerned for Taylor. Either that or he was a damn good actor. "I finished with meetings around eight, then had dinner with my wife, Tammy. We were home all evening."

Hayes grimaced silently. The perfect cover. A wife couldn't testify against her husband.

And from what he'd heard, Tammy Sutton was salivating for her husband to sit in the governor's chair, and would do anything to ensure his success.

Would she lie to protect him if he was a murderer?

TAYLOR'S NERVES PINGED BACK and forth as she and Hayes drove to her estate. She hated putting her friends on the spot and hoped she hadn't damaged their working relationship today. She'd even considered the possibility that someone had framed Kenneth in an effort to degrade his name and throw off the election.

"Exactly what is your relationship with Sutton?" Hayes asked as they entered her house.

Her eyes widened in annoyance. "We work together, Hayes. I respect his decisions and appreciate the fact that he's contributed to several charities."

"What about those illegal bids?"

She bit down on her lip. "I'm still digging through the paper trail to figure out what happened. But I honestly don't think Kenneth would participate in anything illegal. He wouldn't take that chance."

"Not in an election year?" Hayes asked sarcastically.

Taylor grimaced. "Not at any time."

"Sometimes power and greed go to a man's head," Hayes said. "Maybe he thought the end justified the means."

Taylor shrugged, still not buying the supposition. "Just because someone has political aspirations or money doesn't automatically make them bad."

He grunted in disagreement, and she gritted her teeth. "You're too judgmental, Hayes. But you're wrong about Kenneth. He's one of the good guys."

"Sounds as if you're in love with the man," Hayes said darkly.

Taylor whipped her head around in surprise. "No, Hayes. I admire him and think he'll make a great governor, but our relationship is totally professional."

"Really?" he said in a mocking tone. "He doesn't have any indiscretions to hide?"

Anger churned in her stomach at his implications. "Are you asking me if he's having an affair? Or if we've been together?"

Hayes's razor sharp gaze cut through her like a knife.

"No, he's not having an affair, Hayes, and we've *never* slept together," Taylor said. "I do have morals, and I would never sleep with a married man."

His jaw slackened slightly. "So he's happy in his marriage?"

Taylor pressed her fingers to her temple where a headache was starting to pulse. "He and Tammy seem to be in sync. They both have the same goal, Kenneth as governor. And I've never seen them argue." But still, she wasn't sure the love was there, at least not in his eyes. Sure, Tammy was obsessed with being his wife, and with him, but Taylor didn't see the passion she thought should be between a man and woman. The passion she wanted.

The passion she was starting to imagine between her and Hayes.

But she refrained from confiding her opinion. It would only make Kenneth look guilty in Hayes's eyes.

Suddenly his interrogation felt too invasive. He wouldn't talk about himself, but wanted to dissect her life, her friends, her family. Last night and today had taken their toll. She had to escape Hayes's probing eyes and questions. "I have some work to do now."

He simply stared at her, unnerving her even more. "Fine. I need to check in with Brody and Egan."

She nodded, then slipped into her office and shut the door. After downing some aspirin, she spent the afternoon and evening working on the fund-raiser for the teen center, throwing herself into her work and forcing Hayes from her mind as she concentrated on organizing an art auction to raise money.

By seven her stomach growled, and her headache told her she needed food. She hadn't eaten lunch, so she walked to the kitchen and began gathering ingredients for a shrimp stir-fry.

Hayes was working on his laptop at the table, and she began chopping vegetables. When she glanced up, he was watching her, his eyebrows arched, his look hooded. "I figured you had a gourmet chef on staff."

She laughed, but her huge kitchen seemed smaller now with him in it, more intimate with his big body taking up so much space. His masculine scent wafted around her, stirring other hungers that she couldn't feed. "I do." She tapped her chest. "Me."

He studied her for so long that she wondered at his thoughts.

"You're not exactly what you seem," he finally said in a gruff voice.

His quietly spoken words sent a tiny thrill through her because she knew it had cost him. Because maybe he felt the sexual tension charging the air.

Desire flared between them as they gazed at one another, but he turned away as if the connection between them had caught him off guard. Still, as she finished preparing the meal, the air thickened with his male scent and that odd feeling of intimacy intensified.

When she served him a dish and he dug into it with gusto, a sense of satisfaction filled her that she'd impressed him with her culinary skills. Her mind also took a dangerous journey as she imagined them sipping wine as they listened to music, cuddling on the couch, then slipping up to her suite hand in hand. He'd kiss her and trace his hands over her body, slowly undress her and feed her hunger with his mouth and tongue. And she'd tease him and prime his body for a night of hot lovemaking that would last for hours.

Her cell phone rang from inside her purse, and she was startled, her fork in midair. She didn't want to talk to anyone, didn't want to intrude on the serene moment, but it jangled again, and Hayes sipped his tea, obviously oblivious to her fantasies.

Thank God. The tension of the investigation must be making her insane.

"Aren't you going to answer the phone?" he asked.

She sighed, afraid it might be Miles ranting about their earlier visit. If so, she'd have to stand her ground. Clenching her hands, she crossed to the desk in the corner, removed the phone from her purse, then checked the number on the caller ID. Tony Morris, the private investigator she'd hired to locate information on the baby Margaret had given up for adoption years ago.

She grabbed the handset and walked to the living room out of earshot.

"Miss Landis," a deep baritone voice said, "I have that information you requested."

She inhaled sharply, running her fingers along the mantel as she glanced at a photograph of her and Margaret taken at a Christmas charity function. Margaret had talked about her baby that night, of all the holidays and birthdays she'd missed.

Nerves pinged inside her.

What if finding Margaret's child somehow caused Margaret more pain?

Chapter Seven

"Miss Landis, are you there?"

Taylor's breath gushed out. "Yes. Did you find out what happened to Miss Hathaway's baby?"

"Yes," Morris said. "The infant Miss Hathaway gave birth to was placed with a couple in San Antonio. Their name was Keller."

"Keller?" Taylor staggered slightly. She couldn't have heard him right.

"Yes, Keller. Apparently someone paid them to take the child, and they didn't officially adopt him. They'd lost a son of their own, and never really connected with this boy. He got into some trouble as a teen and left home at seventeen."

Taylor's heart thumped madly in her chest. "What was the child's name?"

"They named the little boy Hayes."

The room spun sickeningly. It couldn't be possible, could it?

Hayes was her best friend's son?

"Do you have definitive proof?" Taylor rasped.

"Yes, I can fax it over—"

"No, no, don't do that." She couldn't chance anyone seeing the confidential information.

"Then we'll meet in person."

"Yes, that's better."

Footfalls clattered on the floor and Hayes appeared in the doorway, his brow furrowed.

What should she do now? She couldn't tell Hayes—he despised her and Margaret's lifestyle. How would he react if he learned Margaret had given him away? That her fortunes could be his own? That he could have grown up in Cantara Hills with so much more than he'd had?

And what about Margaret? How would she feel when she discovered the baby she'd given up, the one she'd pined for for years, the one she wanted to meet, was the brooding ranger who'd been staying in Cantara Hills? The man who was playing Taylor's bodyguard and would be following her every day as Margaret planned her wedding to Devon Goldenrod?

Margaret's father had assured her the child had been placed in a loving home, that the baby was better off being raised by two loving parents instead of a teenage girl, that he'd checked on him over the years and assured Margaret he'd led a picture-perfect life, that all his needs had been met and he'd wanted for nothing.

But he'd either been mistaken or he'd lied.

SOMETHING WAS WRONG. Taylor's face had turned bone-white.

And as she disconnected the call, her hand trembled and she jammed it through her hair.

He had the oddest urge to pull her in his arms, to

soothe her and assure her everything would be all right. But he remained rooted at the doorway, knowing if he did, he'd be crossing that invisible line that divided the two of them so distinctly in his mind. The one built by money and culture. "What's wrong, Taylor?"

Her breath whispered out. "Nothing."

He strode to her, then gripped her by the arms. "Then why do you look as if you just saw a ghost?"

She shook her head in denial, but she refused to look him in the eye. "I'm fine…."

He tipped her chin up with his thumb. "Then why won't you look at me?"

Her throat worked as she swallowed, drawing his gaze to the slender column of her neck. Damn. Her skin looked so incredibly soft, and it would probably taste like sin.

He hadn't tasted sin in a long time.

"What's going on, Taylor? Who was that on the phone?"

"Nobody," she said a little too quickly, rousing his curiosity even more.

"Don't lie to me. You're upset. Was it your brother or Sutton?"

Again she shook her head. "No, no, neither of them."

His mouth thinned. "Someone who threatened you?"

She pulled away, rubbing her arms where he'd gripped them, and regret slammed into his stomach. Had he hurt her? Been holding her too roughly?

"No, nothing like that." She paced to the Palladian window and stared outside. Night was falling, shades of gray slanting in shadows across the manicured lawn. He felt himself falling into those shades of gray himself, wanting to be her friend, to take care of her, when he needed to keep her at a distance just to guard himself.

"Taylor, it's my job to protect you and find out who tried to kill you," he said as much to remind himself as to convince her to talk. "I can't do that if you're not honest with me. Tell me what's going on."

When she turned to him, her eyes glittered with wariness and other emotions he couldn't read. "The call was personal business, Hayes. I swear, it had nothing to do with the attack on me."

"Maybe you should tell me and let me decide."

She shook her head. "No…it's not important, just some news about an old friend that took me off guard."

He narrowed his eyes, searching her face for the truth. But all he saw were lies.

Dammit, just when he'd begun to halfway think she was different from the other rich girls, that she was someone he could trust and like, she proved him wrong.

TAYLOR HATED TO LIE TO HAYES, but she couldn't very well confide the truth. Not now.

Not yet.

She had to talk to Margaret first. This was Margaret's secret to share, not hers. And Margaret would have to decide how she wanted to handle the situation, if and when she wanted to tell Hayes about his birth.

Worry knotted her insides, and she knew she had to escape. Hayes's look of disappointment ripped at her conscience. Relinquishing her privacy for a bodyguard was difficult enough, but trusting him with her emotions and Margaret's secret was impossible.

Men just wanted money or sex, not love.

Although Hayes seemed to want none of them from her....

But occasionally she noticed a spark of sexual interest flare in his eyes. Desire that he quickly hid.

Disturbed by his presence even more now after learning he was Margaret's son, she rushed to the sink to clean up from their meal. She needed to do something, keep busy, to occupy her confused mind and prevent her from acting on her raging hormones.

As she began to gather the dinner plates, he took them from her. "You cooked. I clean up. That was the rule at my house."

Her heart squeezed. "You're not there anymore," she said, feeling the slow burn of tears sting her eyes. He should never have been in that home, never suffered, felt unwanted....

His jaw tightened. "Taylor, look at me." His voice was so gruff that a tingle rippled through her. She didn't want to see the pain of his past in his eyes.

"You look exhausted," he said. "Let me take care of the kitchen, and you lie down."

"I'm fine," she said, although her protests sounded feeble to her own ears. She wanted to make him see that Margaret loved him and regretted giving him up, so everything would be all right.

Then she'd hold him and kiss him, and feel his lips on hers all night.

"No, you're not fine," he said more gently. "You just came home from the hospital this morning, and it's been a stressful day. Go on to bed."

His dark brooding gaze raked over her, and for a second, they connected again, and heat flickered in his eyes. She didn't want to go to bed alone. Was afraid she'd dream about that man trying to strangle her in her swimming pool.

But she couldn't ask Hayes to comfort her. Not when the secret she carried lay lodged in her throat like a rock. So she nodded, then disappeared up the steps.

Inside her room, she paced like an animal, her nerves tightening her throat, making it impossible to breathe. She was so agitated she couldn't sleep.

She had to know for certain that the information the private investigator had was correct. Tomorrow she and Margaret planned to meet for lunch to discuss wedding plans. If she had the proof in hand, then she could decide whether or not to show Margaret at the time.

She grabbed her cell phone and punched in the detective's number. She'd sneak out tonight, meet him and get that proof. Then she'd decide what to do with it.

HAYES LOADED THE DISHWASHER, his mouth watering over the delicious meal Taylor had prepared, his mind chasing suspicions about why the phone call had disturbed her. Who had been on the phone? Was she lying about the news pertaining to an old friend?

Maybe an old boyfriend had called?

For some reason that thought disturbed him, but when he'd asked her earlier if she had a boyfriend who might want to harm her, she'd denied it vehemently.

Hell, if the caller had phoned in on the landline, he could check the number for himself.

He needed to win her trust so he could extract the truth.

He finished stowing the dishes, then phoned Egan.

Two rings later, Egan answered. "How's it going babysitting the princess?"

He'd used that expression before himself, but hearing Egan say it grated on his nerves. "Fine. Did you hear anything from trace on the crime scene last night?"

"That hair you found belonged to Tammy Sutton."

"Hell, that doesn't do us much good. Taylor said Tammy is over here all the time. In fact, all our major players have been in this house for charity functions and other reasons during the past few weeks."

"I know, it's frustrating," Egan said. "What about you? You come up with anything?"

"We had a chat with Miles Landis. The punk is so spoiled he thinks his daddy will bail him out no matter what he does."

"I'm sure his daddy would," Egan said.

"Yeah, but if Miles tried to kill Taylor, he's not getting away with it."

"Did he have an alibi?"

"No," Hayes replied. "Claimed he was at the clubs, got drunk and passed out."

"Sounds like his routine," Egan said. "What about Sutton?"

"Sutton insists he was at a meeting until eight. Then he went home to the loving wife. So far his story checks out, but his wife is his alibi, so who knows?"

Egan barked a laugh. "Yeah, she loves money and power and knows how to obtain both."

"Right. Either way, if Sutton is our man, I don't see us turning Tammy." Another dead end. Hayes explained about Margaret Hathaway's upcoming wedding and Taylor's involvement.

"So I guess you'll be shopping for bridesmaid's dresses and flowers with Taylor," Egan said on a roar of laughter.

Hayes grimaced. Spending any time with Taylor and these country club women was torture, but to look at bridal stuff sucked big-time.

And Margaret Hathaway…something about that woman had thrown him off balance. She'd stood up to him just like Taylor had—in fact, he could see why they were friends. Both were attractive glitzy women with wealth and…dedicated to charity work. So were Victoria Kirkland and Caroline Stallings, two more Cantara Hills residents, and the women Brody and Egan had fallen for.

Frustrated, he hung up and paced the living area, itching to know who Taylor had talked to earlier and why she had withheld information from him.

Muscles coiled with tension, he checked the security system, then stretched out on the sofa, hoping to catch some sleep. The night before he certainly hadn't, not in that hospital room where Taylor lay a few feet away.

He closed his eyes and was about to doze off when the sound of a car engine sputtering to life startled him. It was Taylor's car.

Dammit, she was sneaking out. Where in the hell was she going this late at night?

He raced to the door to stop her, but he heard the automatic garage door shutting, and realized it was too late.

Maybe she had a secret lover she hadn't told him about and she'd gone to meet him. Or maybe the killer had phoned her for a rendezvous.

Anger railed inside him as he hurried to his car to follow her.

TAYLOR FELT LIKE A THIEF sneaking out in the night as she revved up her ice-blue Mercedes convertible and sped toward the private detective's office in San Antonio. Traffic was mild for the night, but the temperature had skyrocketed, the heat making her clothes stick to her skin. Still, she loved the freedom riding with the top down offered. A slight breeze tossed her hair around her face, then she noticed headlights zooming closer on her tail.

Was someone following her?

Nerves fluttered in her stomach, and she considered turning around or calling Hayes. But what could she tell him? That she was going to meet a private investigator about him?

As she rounded a curve, she noticed the car had fallen back several hundred yards. Relief surged through her. But she continued to check until she reached the city and the private detective's office. The building was nondescript and dark, except for a low light burning through a darkly tinted window. Her breath tight in her chest, she hurried to the door. Morris had promised he'd wait on her, so she knocked, then eased inside.

The door screeched and the inside light flickered off. Then a shot rang out, glass shattered from the front window and spewed across the room.

Taylor dove to the floor and screamed, crawling on her hands and knees behind the desk just as another bullet hit the carpet beside her.

Chapter Eight

Hayes heard the gunfire, removed his weapon from his shoulder holster and eased up to the door of the P.I.'s office. What in the hell was going on? Who was firing?

Was Taylor hit?

Darkness shrouded the interior and he inched inside, pausing to scan the shadows. The sound of choppy breathing echoed in the silence, mingling with his own raging heart, and he searched the darkness again but saw nothing.

Outside, a car engine screeched to life, tires squealing as the vehicle lurched from the curb. He ran to the door, but all he could discern were the taillights of a dark sedan spinning around the corner.

He wanted to chase after it, but had to find Taylor. Hurrying back to the door, once again he scanned the office interior.

"Oh, God…"

"Taylor?"

She peeked from behind the desk, her silhouette a trembling shadow against the faint streetlight slanting through the blinds. "Hayes?"

"Yeah, are you all right?"

A whimper tore from her throat. "Yes, is he gone?"

"Yeah." Anger and fear knotted his insides, and he crossed the room to her, his boots clacking on the floor.

"Hayes," Taylor whispered, "there's a b-body here."

He glanced down at her feet and spotted a man sprawled behind the desk. The scent of blood and death rose to greet him, but he felt for a pulse. "It's too late," he said with a curse.

She whimpered in shock, and he grabbed her, pulling her away from the corpse. "What happened, Taylor?"

"I came in, but someone started shooting." Her voice broke, the horror of finding the man evident as a sob escaped her.

Gritting his teeth, he dragged her into his arms, pressed her head against his shoulder and soothed her. "Shh, it's okay."

"No…" she whispered. "He's dead."

"I know, but you're all right," he said, his own breathing choppy as he moved her to a chair in the corner and eased her into it. "I have to call it in, Taylor."

She nodded against him, clinging to his shirt, and he held her tighter, well aware of his heart pounding in his chest. If something had happened to her…

No, he couldn't think like that. Taylor hadn't been hit.

On the heels of fear, anger shot through him. Before he called it in, he had to know what had happened, why she was meeting a P.I. in the night.

"You know this man?" he asked gruffly.

Her body stiffened, and he searched her face. "Who is he, Taylor? Why did you sneak out to meet him?"

"His name is Morris," she said feebly.

"He's a private investigator?"

She nodded, averting her gaze to stare at the body, and he trapped her face between his hands. "What were you doing here?"

Her breath rushed out, but she didn't answer.

"Taylor," he said more harshly. "Answer me. What's going on?"

She clamped her teeth over her bottom lip, shaking her head as if to deny him, and pure rage knotted his insides.

"Listen to me," he rasped. "Someone tried to kill you last night, and you're in my custody. If you're in some kind of trouble, if you know why someone wants you dead, you have to tell me."

"I really don't know," she said in a low voice.

"Why were you meeting this P.I.?" he asked again, more demanding this time.

"I can't tell you that," she said.

He released her abruptly, furious. "Why not?"

"Because it's personal," she cried.

"Is it business? Related to your father's foundation?" He hesitated. "Or personal as in a lover you forgot to mention?"

Her head moved from side to side, her face pale in the dim light. "No, nothing like that. It's…not about me."

"Then tell me," he shouted.

A strained second passed between them. "I can't," she finally said, then turned away from him and folded her arms around herself as if to shut him out completely.

Frustrated and furious with her, he phoned Egan to explain the situation.

"I'll get a crime unit there," Egan said. "Find out why Taylor Landis needed that P.I."

"I will," he said. Although he didn't know how he'd do that. She'd clammed up and was refusing to talk.

But this was the second time in two days she'd nearly died. And judging from the timing of their little midnight rendezvous, this man's death had to be related to her visit.

TAYLOR TREMBLED, THE SIGHT of the blood pooling beneath Morris's chest so vivid that nausea rippled through her.

Did his death have something to do with the information he'd revealed to her on the phone? If so, she had to confide in Hayes and the police. But her loyalty lay with her best friend.

Fear clogged her throat. Hayes's face was a mask of fury as he greeted the crime scene unit, medical examiner and a local unit.

CSI began to process the scene, dusting for fingerprints, looking for trace evidence, and Hayes and a local officer approached her.

"Miss Landis, I'm Lieutenant Riley. Ranger Keller said that you and he found the body."

Hayes's gaze met hers, and she realized that he'd implied they'd arrived together. Her mind raced with how to answer, but she simply nodded.

"What were you doing here this time of night?" Lieutenant Riley asked.

She glanced at Hayes again, his jaw tense as he waited on her reply. "Mr. Morris called me and said that he had some information he wanted to give me."

"What kind of information?" he asked.

She chewed the inside of her cheek. "He didn't get a chance to give it to me."

"Was he working for you?" the lieutenant asked.

Again she hedged. Technically the investigation was for Margaret. "No."

His brow furrowed, and Hayes's eyes flickered with questions.

"Was he blackmailing you?" Lieutenant Riley asked.

She shook her head. "No. Like I said, he phoned me and said he had information to give me. When I arrived, someone shot at me. I ducked behind the desk and that's when I found his b-body."

The lieutenant gestured toward Hayes. "Ranger Keller said that someone also tried to kill you last night."

She shivered, then murmured that he was correct.

"And you don't have any idea why?"

"No."

One of the crime scene investigators approached, saving her from a lengthier interrogation. "Please don't leave town, Miss Landis," Riley said. "We may need to talk to you again."

She nodded, her hands tightening together as the investigator showed Hayes and the lieutenant a bullet casing he'd found by the doorway. "Looks like a .38."

"We'll bag it and send it to forensics," the investigator said.

Hayes squatted down, then removed a handkerchief and used it to pick up a small brass button with black etching on it that had rolled beneath the desk chair. "This might have come from our guy. Maybe from some kind of uniform?"

Riley bent to study it, as well. "The killer and Morris could have struggled first, and the button fell off, then the killer shot Morris."

"We'll send it to trace." The investigator bagged it.

Hayes pressed his hand to her shoulder. "Taylor, they need to take your prints for elimination purposes."

A numbness crept over her as she agreed.

Had this man died because of another case or because he'd dug into the past for her? If Hayes and the police searched Morris's files, would they find papers proving that Hayes was Margaret's son?

Dear heavens, she had to talk to Margaret and convince her to tell Hayes that she'd given birth to him. It would be difficult enough for both of them to handle the realization, but it would be far worse if Hayes learned his mother's identity from Morris's files instead of from Margaret.

"WHEN CSI IS FINISHED, I WANT Morris's files and computer sent to me at Miss Landis's house in Cantara Hills," Hayes told the lieutenant. "Maybe one of his cases got him murdered."

Taylor gave him a wary look, but Riley nodded. "Just keep me abreast of anything you discover."

Hayes assured the lieutenant he would keep in touch. The button might prove instrumental in solving their case, especially if they identified the type of uniform it had come from. Hopefully, they'd find prints or DNA that would lead to the killer.

Although he'd vouched for Taylor in front of the lieutenant, anger still fueled his demeanor as he followed her back to her estate. He had to push her, find out what that P.I. had wanted with her.

Because he strongly sensed that she was lying. That the private investigator had revealed his discovery to her on the phone.

Had that information brought a murderer to his door?

If so, why? The foundation business? The bids for the city council? Dirt on her brother? On her?

She pulled the sleek little convertible into the garage, hitting the automatic button to lower the door. He parked in the drive, a reminder that he didn't fit into her world and never would.

Was that the reason she wouldn't trust him with the truth?

She let him inside the front door, and he itched to pounce on her with questions, but the sight of the dark circles beneath her eyes made his gut clench.

"You look wiped out, Taylor."

"I am. I'm going to bed now."

He caught her arm before she could disappear up the stairs. "And this time stay there. No more sneaking out."

Fear flickered in her eyes, and she shook her head, her chin quivering. "Don't worry, Hayes. I won't. I…I'm sorry."

He didn't know if she was apologizing for sneaking out or lying about the P.I., and he didn't ask. But if she tried to sneak out again, he'd handcuff her to the bed and park himself in the room with her.

That thought triggered unbidden images he couldn't pursue, but they fed his libido anyway, making him even more frustrated.

Dammit. He needed to find the person after Taylor so he could get the hell out of Cantara Hills. He didn't want this simmering attraction to her.

Knowing he couldn't do any more tonight, he booted up his computer and ran a search on the button. Image after image of various uniforms spilled onto the screen, and he scanned the pictures.

Police uniforms, paramedics, firemen, postal and UPS workers, military uniforms, power company employees…the pictures continued. Finally an hour into the search he discovered a similar-looking button.

He clicked on the icon to enlarge the image, frowning as he recognized the crisp navy color, the hat, the row of shiny round brass buttons with black etching along the lapel—a chauffeur uniform.

His mind spun with jumbled thoughts of where he'd seen one like it before. The company that made it was based in Austin.

His throat thickened as recognition dawned. Egan's father, Walt, was Link Hathaway's chauffeur and wore an identical uniform.

But why would Walt be at a private investigator's office?

He wouldn't.…

Perhaps he was covering for Link Hathaway. He was loyal to the man to a fault.

No. It had to be someone else. Another chauffeur who wore the same type of uniform.

But what if it wasn't? Would forensics be able to lift a print? And if they found out it belonged to Walt, what motive would he have to kill Morris, or Taylor?

He reached for the phone to call Egan, but decided to wait until he had some answers first. He couldn't accuse Egan's father without more proof. If he did, Egan would never forgive him.

When the case was solved, he had to make amends with his friends. Taylor wouldn't be a part of his life, but Egan and Brody had to be.

They were his only family.

TAYLOR CLIMBED IN THE SHOWER, desperately wishing she could wash away the images of the dead man's face as she scrubbed the scent of death from her body. Barring an occasional funeral, she'd never seen a dead person before, not in the first few moments when life had been snatched from them. Especially a life lost to violence.

Morris's wide gray eyes had stared up at her, and as she crawled along the floor, she'd brushed his skin. It had felt warm yet oddly like ice. And the smell…

Nausea gripped her, and she swallowed hard, willing it to pass as she leaned against the shower door and heaved for a breath. Hayes must see death all the time in his job. How did he handle it?

The water grew cold, and she flipped it off, dried off and bundled in her bathrobe. The air conditioner whirred, sending a chill through her. She hurried to the closet, pulled out a satin gown and slid it on, then climbed into bed, dragging the covers over her.

Exhausted, she closed her eyes but didn't think she'd sleep. Yet she was so drained and spent physically and emotionally that she slowly drifted off. But her sleep was fitful, and she jerked awake sometime later with a scream.

She'd felt a man's hands sliding around her throat, his fingers tightening, strangling her. Then the image of Morris's bloody body had floated in front of her, only his face faded to a dull black.

Then hers replaced it.

Chapter Nine

At the sound of Taylor's cry, fear bolted through Hayes, and he raced up the steps to her bedroom. His gun drawn, he pushed open the door and searched the darkness. Moonlight shimmered through the window, casting a golden glow on the room. Taylor bolted upright to a sitting position, gasping for a breath as she pressed her hands to her chest.

"Taylor?"

"I'm sorry," she whispered hoarsely. "Bad dream."

Her voice caught, and his gut clenched. As angry as he'd been with her earlier, he'd recognized the shock in her eyes at the sight of Morris's dead body.

She was terrified but trying desperately not to show it.

Forgetting all rational sense, he strode toward her, placed his gun on her nightstand, lowered himself onto the mattress and pulled her into his arms. She fell against him, a soft, satiny female puddle of sexuality and vulnerability, and his body hardened as he admitted to himself how much he'd been wanting to hold her.

And taste her and touch her.

"I saw that man in my dreams, and all that blood,"

she whispered, "and then it was me, my face, my blood…"

"It's not you," he murmured.

She touched her neck. "I could feel hands around my throat choking me."

"Shh, it's over," he murmured. Her hair tickled his cheek and he stroked her back, cradling her in his arms. "You're safe now, Taylor. I've got you."

"I can't believe this is happening," she said on a sob. "First Kimberly dying, then someone attacking Victoria and Caroline."

And now her.

Someone definitely had targeted the women in Cantara Hills. Victoria Kirkland had been targeted because she'd freed her client from charges of trying to kill Kimberly, and she'd helped Ranger McQuade investigate. Then Carlson Woodward had tried to kill Caroline. Did it all lead back to Kimberly's murder, or was he right to suspect Miles or Kenneth Sutton? Although why would one of them murder the private investigator?

Only Taylor could tell him.

Or the man's files. Tomorrow…

The sweet scent of her bodywash and shampoo, something utterly feminine and sexy as hell, wafted to him, as she burrowed herself in his arms. "I don't want to go back to sleep," she said softly. "I'm afraid I'll see that man's eyes staring up at me. And his body was so cold…."

She shivered against him, so fragile that every primal male bone in his body screamed to protect her, to erase her fears and pain and replace that terror with other sensations. Pleasurable ones. Like his hands stroking her. His mouth tasting hers.

Just a taste.

Not a relationship, but just one sweet taste of her delicious lips.

"Don't think about it," he said in a husky whisper.

"How do you do it, Hayes? How do you deal with death all the time?"

"It's a job," he said. "I don't get close or let it get personal."

Except it felt personal right now.

Her breasts rose and fell, her soft mounds teasing his hard chest, eliciting wicked fantasies. His sex hardened, straining against his fly as he felt her curves beneath the softness of her gown. A gown that was so paper-thin that her nipples budding to life stirred his desires and made his breath catch.

He had to leave. Remove himself from her presence before he did something foolish like kiss her.

He started to pull away, but she clutched his shirt, then lifted her hands to cup his face. The rasp of his beard stubble sounded like sandpaper as her delicate fingers touched him, but he didn't have the power to move.

"Don't go, Hayes. Stay with me."

He closed his eyes, hating himself and the fact that he wanted her. That he was too weak to deny her or himself a moment of passion.

Still, somewhere he dredged up enough stamina to lift his hands and press them over hers. He meant to pry them loose, but instead she flicked out her tongue and traced it along the seam of his lips.

"Taylor—"

She shushed him this time by pressing her mouth to his jaw, then she nibbled her way to his mouth, and he opened for her, taking everything she offered as he claimed her mouth with his.

TAYLOR KNEW SHE WAS PLAYING with fire, but she wanted to forget the horrible reality that had become her life. That her brother and friends were suspects and might be trying to hurt her. That tonight she had been touched by death again, and had escaped it herself by mere seconds. That an inch closer and that bullet would have pierced her heart and her blood would have been spilled across the floor, her life over.

That tomorrow she had to tell Margaret she'd found her son, and that Hayes might find out and it would give him another reason to detest her and Margaret.

For now, all she wanted to do was taste the sinfully sexy curve of his lips and feel his hard, tough body against her.

His kiss consumed her, demanding and urgent with need, and her stomach fluttered with desire. He raked one hand through her hair, while the other one slid along her spine, pressing her more tightly against the manly planes of his sculpted body. He probed her lips apart with his tongue, slid it inside and teased her, showing no mercy as he thrust deeper inside her mouth.

Heat speared her, making her nipples hard buds, tight, heavy, achy. She wanted his hands and mouth on her.

Like a cat, she purred into his mouth and rubbed herself against him, stoking the fire burning between them. As if he sensed the depth of her need, his hand encased her, kneading her weight, and an intense hunger sizzled from her breasts to her womb, igniting hidden desires and enflaming her senses with heat.

Desperate to strip him and feel his naked body gliding against hers, she lifted her hand to his chest and slowly unbuttoned the top button of his shirt. He groaned, then trailed kisses along the column of her neck. She threw her head back in abandon, whispering that she wanted him, and he licked his way down her throat, then untied the ribbon at the top of her gown, parting the satin so he could close his mouth over her tight nipple. Searing fire raced along her bare flesh, his sucking spiking the flames of desire to an inferno.

She dug her hands into his hair, holding him closer as he teased the bud with his tongue, sweeping his lips across her skin with nibbling bites that made her grow wet and warm and needy all over.

She craved more.

"Hayes…" She clawed at him, anxious, achy, throbbing for his full length to thrust inside her, stretching her, filling her, sating her.

Greedily, she ripped at his shirt, sending buttons flying then ran her hands across his bare chest. He moved his hand to her thigh, and she groaned his name.

"Please, Hayes, I need you…."

Suddenly his cell phone trilled, the sound shrill and vibrating between them like a whistle signaling the end of an exciting train ride before the train had reached its destination.

She caught his hand when he started to pull away, anxious that he ignore it and let them finish the ride together. "No, don't stop, please, Hayes—"

The phone trilled again, though, and he tore his mouth from her breast with a guttural groan, and looked up at her, his ragged breathing slicing the air between them as he checked the number.

"Dammit, it's your father." He growled and stood, putting distance between them.

"Don't answer it," Taylor whispered. "Come back to bed with me, Hayes. We can be good together."

She knew she sounded pathetic, and had never begged a man to make love to her. But she'd never wanted a man like she did Hayes.

She ached all over, felt empty and hungry inside. Her gown lay open, her nipples tight and wet from his tongue, her breasts heavy mounds that needed more, her skin a burning flame that needed stoking, her mouth watering to taste his salty skin, to close her lips around his throbbing member and lave him with her tongue.

He couldn't leave her like this.

But he did. He grabbed his gun, strode from the room, his boots pounding on the staircase as he charged from her bedroom away from her.

HAYES CURSED, HIS BODY throbbing like the devil as he rushed down the stairs. His phone jangled again, and he yanked it from his belt and answered. "Keller."

"Yes, this is Lionel Landis. I apologize for calling so late, but I tried to reach Taylor earlier and there was no answer. Is she all right?"

Hayes ground his teeth at the man's formal tone. Taylor's father would dismiss him if he knew what he'd been doing with his daughter. "Taylor is fine," he said instead. In fact, she was more than fine. She was erotic as hell, and he wanted to run back up to her room, crawl in bed with her and make love to her until neither of them had the energy to walk.

Landis cleared his throat. "And the investigation?"

"We're still working on it."

"Do you have any suspects, Keller?"

Yes, your son, and Kenneth Sutton, who the man was probably buddy-buddy with. "I can't discuss the details of the case, but I'll let you know when we make an arrest."

"All right," Landis said curtly. "But, Keller, you'd better take good care of my little girl. If anything happens to her, you'll answer to me."

And Landis would use his power and money to make trouble for him. "Yes, sir," he said through gritted teeth. As if he needed a reminder of the different stations between him and Landis's precious daughter. "Don't worry."

Landis hung up, and Hayes cursed and walked out back to the swimming pool for fresh air, but the image of Taylor floating facedown, near death, haunted him.

He was here as her bodyguard. Not as her lover.

He needed to have his ass kicked for forgetting for one moment that he was the hired hand, that sleeping with Taylor would be a big fat mistake.

He lifted his hand to his badge. His badge was all that mattered. It was his life. The only reason he was in Cantara Hills was because Kimberly had been murdered and someone was after Taylor.

He wished to hell he had that P.I.'s files tonight. He needed something to do to keep his mind off of what had happened between him and Taylor.

Because her scent still lingered on his skin, her taste on his tongue, and he wanted more of her.

TAYLOR WOKE THE NEXT MORNING, agitated and irritable. She'd felt cold and vulnerable when Hayes had stormed from her bed without looking back, and more than a little confused by his withdrawal. Normally when stressed, she'd take her frustrations out in the swimming pool, but the memory of the attack sent a shiver through her.

Only Hayes could assuage this ache.

And he had wanted her. His body had been hard and pumped, his frenzied hands and mouth as anxious for her as she had been for him.

So why had he stopped?

And why had she begged him not to?

Because she was a fool. Hayes was a Texas Ranger, a man who didn't get involved, who hated her lifestyle and friends. How many times and ways did he have to tell her that?

Sure, his body had been primed for her, but what man would have turned down an offer of free, unattached sex? For all she knew, he had a woman—or maybe a dozen women—waiting on him when he left Cantara Hills.

Humiliation stung her cheeks as she showered and dressed. She could not have a repeat episode. Her self-confidence couldn't endure another rejection.

Besides, it was better that he'd halted before they'd made love. When he learned Margaret was his mother, and that Taylor had lied to him about hiring the private investigator, he would probably hate them both.

She twisted her hair into a low knot, added her diamond earrings and watch, then checked the time. Today she was meeting Margaret. Her stomach fluttered. She had to tell her about Hayes.

How would Margaret react?

Worse, how would she have felt if Taylor had slept with her son?

Good heavens, why was she so attracted to him anyway? They had nothing in common.

Nothing except…maybe that was what she liked about him. He wasn't interested in her money. Didn't want anything to do with her society life.

He was strong, protective, courageous. Rugged.

A cowboy.

God, he looked good in that Stetson.

Her stomach tightened. She'd like to see him wearing nothing but that hat. Her nipples jutted with arousal at the thought, a warm wetness tickling her thighs. He'd tip it low over those eyes, eyes framed by thick black lashes and brows, eyes that would watch her with passion beneath the hat brim as she slowly undressed for him.

Downstairs, his boots clattered on the marble floor, jerking her from her fantasy, and she pursed her lips, wondering how he'd fared after their interlude, if he'd fantasized about her instead of sleeping.

Evil thoughts speared her. She hoped he'd been horny as hell and had ached all night after leaving her unsated.

Sucking in a sharp breath, she checked the clock and realized she needed to hurry. She and Margaret had a dress fitting at ten, then lunch at the country club.

The intercom for the alarm buzzed, and she rushed to answer it, first glancing at the security camera to identify her visitor. A courier with a package, so she pushed the button to open the gate.

Hayes met her at the front door with a dark look in his eyes. "You just buzzed someone in?"

"A courier," she said.

"What if it was someone pretending to be a courier?"

She chewed her lip, feeling chastised. She hadn't thought of that. "I recognized his uniform."

She opened the door and accepted the package, her heart stuttering as Hayes took the envelope and examined it.

"It's not a bomb," she said, taking it back. "Just papers."

He narrowed his eyes but she simply smiled, then retreated to her office to examine the contents. It was the information from the private investigator. He must have had his mail sent out before he was shot. Inside she found Hayes's birth certificate and papers Margaret and her father had signed relinquishing custody of him. Another document proved that Hayes was Margaret's child, and that he'd been sent to live with a family named Keller.

"Is something wrong?"

She jerked her head up and saw Hayes watching her from the doorway, then jammed the envelope into her shoulder bag. The intensity in his brooding eyes sent a tingle of anxiety and arousal through her.

She wanted to tell him the truth. Wanted to comfort him if the news about Margaret being his mother upset him. Wanted to assure him that Margaret had loved and missed him all through the years.

But she couldn't. "It's fine."

He studied her for another long moment, a flicker of

passion in his eyes as if he was remembering the night before, and her body quivered with longing. She wanted him to touch her again.

"About last night—"

"Don't." She waved a hand, warding off an apology. She had the good sense to know that throwing herself at him had been a mistake.

Unfortunately it didn't make her want him any less or douse the heat lingering between them.

Then his gaze changed, an emotionless hard mask sliding back into place, the walls between them being erected. "I'm hoping to receive those files from the P.I. today. What's on your agenda?"

"I have to meet Margaret for a dress fitting and then lunch."

He gave a clipped nod. "All right, I'll drive."

"That's not necessary," she said, knowing the day would be awkward enough already.

His frown deepened, drawing fine lines around his sexy, brooding mouth. "I promised your father I'd take care of you, Taylor, and I'm going to do my job."

But nothing else. The unspoken words lay between them.

Distress laced his eyes, though, as he followed her to the car. She dreaded the talk with Margaret, but it would be even more uncomfortable knowing Hayes was watching.

Chapter Ten

Hayes gritted his teeth as Taylor exited the fitting room wearing a strapless, satin, sky-blue dress that dipped halfway to her navel. He'd imagined that babysitting her while she and Margaret tried on dresses would be painful, but the sight of her breasts spilling out of the rows of glittering sequins literally made him physically ache.

"What do you think, Margaret?" She twirled around, revealing the back of the dress which also dipped downward to the curve of her hips, tiny crisscrossing strips of fabric showcasing the skin beneath.

"It fits perfectly and enhances your eyes," Margaret said. "And you can wear the green one to the party."

Hayes grimaced. The damn dress would bring out the tongue-wagging men, as well, and have them salivating at her sequined-covered feet.

Her gaze shot to his, where he stood to the side of the dressing rooms, feeling and looking like an awkward outsider.

"What do you think, Hayes?"

Holy hell. She might as well be naked.

A devilish light flickered in her eyes. The conniving

woman was well aware of what the sight of her in that near-nothing fabric was doing to him.

Memories of the night before assaulted him, when his mouth had suckled her, when his tongue had bathed her nipple, when he'd almost slid his fingers all the way up her thigh and taken them both to heaven.

He couldn't forget the sweet taste of her skin or her sultry voice inviting him into her bed, the way she parted her thighs, the way his fingers itched to be inside her.

How the hell was he going to do his job when all he wanted was to take her someplace, strip her and crawl inside her?

TAYLOR TOOK A MODICUM of delight in watching Hayes squirm. She pranced in front of the wall of mirrors, swaying her hips and purposely adjusting the straps of the dress to reveal more cleavage. Her nipples felt sensitive as the fabric rubbed against them, stiff points visible through the sheer fabric.

His look darkened.

She smiled at him in wicked delight. It served him right for abandoning her in the bedroom the night before.

But Margaret emerged from the dressing room wearing her wedding gown, decimating any romantic thoughts about Hayes. Her friend looked stunning in the strapless designer dress with overlays of brocade and lace, and a bodice that curved Margaret's gorgeous figure.

Tears stung Taylor's eyes as Margaret paraded in front of the mirror. Margaret had been alone so long; she wanted her friend to be happy. Taylor only hoped that Devon Goldenrod was as sincere in his affections for her friend as he appeared.

Something niggled at the back of her mind, worrying her, but she couldn't quite put her finger on it.

Hayes leaned against the wall near the mirrors, looking bored and completely out of his element. Yet for a brief second, she imagined modeling a wedding gown for him, and a sharp pang of longing rippled through her. She had grown cynical about men after her few disastrous experiences and had given up on marriage.

Would she ever find a man to love her, not her money and the power afforded by marrying into the Landis family?

"You like the gown, Taylor?" Margaret asked.

Taylor put aside her own selfish thoughts in lieu of her friend. "You look amazing, Margaret. Devon is lucky to have you."

Margaret hugged her, and they chatted about wedding plans for the next few minutes. Hayes yawned, and any fantasies of a possible future with him died.

Dread cramped her stomach, the slow burn of trepidation tightening her lungs as she and Margaret changed, then Hayes drove her to lunch.

Neither spoke on the drive to the country club. She was too nervous about the luncheon, and he was obviously bored out of his mind.

She and Margaret chose to sit at their usual corner table by the window, both preferring the view of the rose gardens and fountain to the golf course. Margaret ordered Perrier and a glass of pinot noir while Taylor ordered a glass of dry white wine.

Margaret glanced at Hayes who had stationed himself at another table to allow them privacy. "Okay, what's going on with that ranger, Taylor? Has he discovered your attacker's identity?"

Taylor's stomach fluttered. "No, not yet."

Margaret sipped her wine. "I know it has to be awkward having him in your house. He seems so…angry all the time."

Goodness, this wasn't going to be easy. "That's what I want to talk to you about."

"About Ranger Keller?"

Taylor shrugged. "Yes, well, sort of."

Margaret's eyes widened. "Oh, no, don't tell me you like him?"

She shrugged. "That's not exactly what I wanted to talk to you about." She took a long swallow of her own glass of wine for courage. "You know how you're always talking about finding out more about your child?"

Margaret's smile faltered, and she dabbed at her mouth with her napkin. "Yes."

"Please don't be upset with me, Margaret, but as a wedding present, I thought I'd surprise you so I hired a private investigator to search for your baby."

Margaret's eyes widened, although she hesitated a moment as if debating whether she wanted to know more. Finally a labored sigh escaped her. "Did you find out something?"

Taylor nodded, rubbing at her temple. "Last night the P.I. called me and said he had information. But when I went to see him, someone shot him."

"Oh my Lord." Margaret pressed her hand to her chest.

"Whoever murdered him was still there and shot at me." Taylor shuddered. "But Hayes rushed in and saved me."

Margaret glanced at Hayes again, relief softening the startled look in her eyes. "Well, I must thank him."

Taylor slid her hand over Margaret's. "There's more."

"The information?" Margaret asked. "You know where my child is, Taylor?"

Emotions thickened Taylor's throat as she nodded. Then she removed the envelope and pushed it in front of Margaret. "The information is in there, Margaret."

Margaret's hand shook as she clutched the envelope, her chin quivering. "Oh my gosh, Tay. I've wondered about my baby, thought about finding him so much, but now I don't know if I'm ready."

Taylor gave her a sympathetic look. "I understand, Margaret. And I'm sorry if I've overstepped and done something to hurt you."

Margaret shook her head. "I could never be angry with you," Margaret said. "You're the one person in the world I trust."

Taylor couldn't speak. She felt the same way and would never hurt her friend. But the truth might.

Margaret inhaled deeply, closed her eyes as if in prayer for a moment, then opened them and unfastened the clasp of the envelope. Her chin quivered as she removed the documents and examined them.

"Oh my goodness..." Tears blurred her eyes and she lifted her gaze to Taylor's in question, then glanced at Hayes, shock straining her features.

"I was stunned, too," Taylor said.

Margaret was so overcome with emotions that she leaned her head on her hands, trembling.

"I'm sorry, Margaret," Taylor whispered.

Margaret jumped up and hurried toward the powder room. Taylor folded her napkin and followed, her heart in her throat.

WHAT IN THE HELL WAS GOING ON?

Hayes trailed the women to the ladies' room in confusion. One minute Taylor and Margaret were modeling fancy dresses and drinking wine in celebration, the next Margaret had flown into tears and run to the powder room.

Because of the contents of that envelope. The envelope the courier had delivered this morning.

As he waited outside the door, standing guard, questions darted through his mind. What was in that envelope?

In light of the night before, could it have had something to do with the private investigator's death? Taylor claimed the information was personal. Did it pertain to Margaret instead of Taylor?

Both women worked on several charities and hosted fund-raisers together. Perhaps they'd discovered financial discrepancies? Or something else?

But what?

Another thought struck him, stirring more worry. If the envelope had come from the P.I. and involved Margaret, could she be in danger, as well?

He punched in Brody's number, grateful when he answered on the second ring. "It's Hayes."

"Yeah, what's going on?"

"Will you run a check on Margaret Hathaway, see what you can find out about her and her family?"

"Why? You got a lead?"

Hayes twisted his mouth in thought and explained about the envelope. "I'm not sure. But it might have something to do with that P.I.'s death. Maybe he had some dirt on Margaret and was going to blackmail her, or maybe someone else is." He scratched his head. "Hell, I don't know. It might be about the charity work she does or maybe about Goldenrod, the pretty boy she's going to marry. I just know something's wrong."

"All right. I'll dig around."

Hayes considered mentioning the button he'd found at the crime scene. After all, Egan's father, Walt, worked for Margaret's father. Maybe Walt had something to do with the P.I.'s death. Either way, the rich people in Cantara Hills seemed to have secrets.

Which one of those secrets was worth killing over?

"I CAN'T BELIEVE IT," Margaret cried.

Taylor pulled Margaret into her arms and hugged her, trying to soothe her tears. "I'm so sorry. I didn't mean to hurt you."

Margaret gulped, pulled away and leaned against the vanity, struggling for a breath. Taylor reached for the box of tissues and shoved them into Margaret's hand.

"From the talk around the club, Hayes Keller grew up in a bad home," Margaret sobbed. "If he learns I'm his mother, he'll hate me even more than he seems to now."

Taylor didn't know how to alleviate Margaret's anxiety. Hayes had suffered and had a chip on his shoulder because of being abandoned. "I didn't know whether to tell you or not, Margaret. But then that private investigator was killed last night, and Hayes was there, and he asked to have the man's files sent to him."

Margaret swung her gaze up to Taylor's, panic darkening her eyes. "What?"

"I'm sorry," Taylor whispered. "Hayes wanted to know why I snuck out to meet a private investigator. He even suggested that the man I hired was killed because of the information he had to give me."

The color drained from Margaret's face, her hand trembling as she reached for another tissue. "Do you think that's possible?"

Taylor bit down on her bottom lip. "I don't know. Maybe someone found out I was looking into your child's whereabouts and didn't want us to find that information."

"Good heavens," Margaret said. "What am I going to do?" She leaned over and splashed cold water on her face, then patted it dry with a hand towel. "All this time I've wanted to see my son, wanted to know he was happy. And he's been here in Cantara Hills and I didn't even know him." She turned to Taylor, pain slashing her features. "Maybe it would be better if he never knew the truth...."

Taylor gripped her friend by the arms. "Margaret, he's going to find out. It's only a matter of time before he sees Morris's files. You have to tell him first, instead of letting him read it in a folder from a private investigator."

Another sob caught in Margaret's throat, but she pushed her fist over her mouth to stifle it, a war of tumultuous emotions flickering in her eyes. "You're right, Tay. But I need to talk to my father first and let him know that I intend to tell Hayes the truth." Her voice cracked. "Will you go with me to talk to Father?"

"I'm not sure that's a good idea, Margaret."

"Please," Margaret begged. "I can use the moral support. My father will try to convince me not to tell Hayes."

"But he will find out," Taylor said. "The police are sending Hayes those files."

Margaret's labored breathing rattled in the air. "Right. But I have to tell my father first." Her voice faded. "And then I have to figure out a way to tell Devon, too."

Taylor clenched her hands together. Link Hathaway would do anything to protect Margaret. And from what Margaret had confided over the years, he'd been adamant that she not search for her child.

Her heart pounded as questions pummeled her. Had Link known all along that Hayes was suffering and left him there anyway? How far would he go to make sure that Margaret didn't reconcile with her child?

Chapter Eleven

Hayes paced outside the ladies' room, feeling conspicuous in his jeans and Stetson amongst the rich and snotty. A birdlike woman with platinum-blond hair narrowed her eyes. "Can I help you, sir?"

He tipped his Stetson. He hated this bodyguard job. "No, ma'am, I'm waiting for Miss Landis and Miss Hathaway."

She shrugged, then strolled across the plush rug at the threshold of the doorway.

Others stared, as well, but his dark glare kept them from approaching. Finally Taylor and Margaret emerged. Margaret's eyes were slightly red although the women must have done a repair job with makeup. Margaret Hathaway had a timeless beauty and sophistication yet something about her also seemed soft and...kind.

A kindness that belied her money and station in life.

Although when she looked up at him, her expression crinkled with sadness.

Confused, he fell into step beside Taylor, something moving inside him at the troubled expression lining her face. "What's going on, Taylor?"

"We're leaving. Margaret wants to visit her father."

"Fine. I'll drive you home."

She caught him by the arm. "Actually, I'm going with her."

"Then so am I."

Her shoulders stiffened. "Hayes, I don't think that's a good idea."

He arched a brow, daring her to argue. "I told you that you go nowhere without me. Remember what happened the last time you did?"

Her face paled, and he felt like a jerk for reminding her, but he couldn't forget she was in danger. And she shouldn't, either.

"I'll sign the bill," Margaret said in a shaky voice.

Margaret gave him another odd look, spoke to the waiter, returned and offered Taylor a strained smile. "All right. I'm ready."

Taylor nodded and they followed Margaret to her silver Jaguar, then he and Taylor went to his SUV. Just the sight of his utility vehicle next to Margaret's and the other expensive toys in the parking lot reminded him of the differences between them.

When Taylor settled in and buckled her seat belt, he angled his head toward her. "What was in that envelope, Taylor?"

Her labored breathing reverberated through the small confines of the SUV. "Nothing."

"Don't lie, Taylor. Whatever it was upset Margaret. Was it some kind of threat to you or Margaret?"

Taylor's gaze shifted to look out the window, and she twisted her hands together. "No," she whispered hoarsely.

Tension rattled her voice, and he reached out and laid

a hand over hers. "I can't help you or her if you don't confide in me."

Her eyes looked tortured. "Just drive to Margaret's, Hayes. She and I will explain later."

He studied her for a second, then reluctantly accepted her answer. Whatever was wrong involved Margaret, and she had to discuss it with her father.

Before the day was over, he would find out what was in that file.

GUILT NAGGED AT TAYLOR as Hayes parked in front of Link Hathaway's Spanish mansion. What would Hayes think if he knew he was about to meet his grandfather?

The man who had insisted Margaret give him away. The man who'd lied to her and assured her that Hayes was happy and lived with a loving family.

The man who had enough money that he could have kept Hayes, even if it meant raising him by nannies. The man who probably wouldn't want anything to do with Hayes now.

Link was a formidable man. Driven by guilt over a teenaged pregnancy, Margaret had always had a difficult time standing up to him.

Margaret pulled into the six-car garage, and Hayes parked in front of the impressive mansion, a frown marring his face as they walked up the tiled path to the arched doorway. When they entered, his gaze swept the interior, a scowl deepening the grooves around his mouth as he assessed the imported chandeliers, two-story winding staircase and Spanish decor.

"Mr. Hathaway likes history," she said, earning a sideways look of disdain.

Margaret appeared through a set of double French doors and glanced at Hayes with such longing and pain that Taylor's heart clenched.

"Father's in the study, Taylor. Ranger…H-Hayes," Margaret stammered. "Would you like to sit on the veranda? Elda can bring you something cold to drink."

"I'll wait here," Hayes said, shoulders squared.

She shot a nervous glance toward Taylor, then nodded. "All right. Make yourself comfortable."

He gave them both a look that said that was impossible, and Taylor's stomach churned. As soon as they entered Link Hathaway's office, Taylor sensed he was angry. That perhaps he even knew the reason for this meeting.

But how was that possible? No one knew about the file but her….

Unless the man who'd killed the private investigator had found the files. Would he phone Link if he had? Maybe for blackmail money?

"Father, I just discovered the truth about my baby," Margaret said in a surprisingly strong voice. She dropped the folder from the private investigator onto her father's desk. He glanced at it then up at Margaret, and slanted a furious stare toward Taylor.

"Don't you think we should discuss this in private?" he said sharply.

Margaret shook her head. "Taylor knows everything, Father. She hired a private investigator to find my son. The file came from him."

His thick gray brows drew together as he scowled. "You should have minded your own business, Taylor. Are you trying to ruin my daughter's happiness?"

"I thought I was helping her," Taylor said.

"She knew I wanted to know more about my baby." Margaret folded her arms. "Why did you lie to me, Father? Why did you tell me he was in a happy home when that file proves otherwise?"

Link paced the room, agitated. "I did what I thought was best to protect you and your future."

"But my baby suffered," Margaret cried. "And he was, *is,* your grandson. How could you leave him in a bad situation when we could have taken care of him so much better?"

Link Hathaway's nostrils flared. "You were fifteen years old, Margaret. Just a child, and an immature, irresponsible one at that, or you wouldn't have found yourself pregnant."

Margaret's face crumpled at his harshness. "I was in love with my baby's father."

"Yes, but he was young, too, and in no better position to get married than you were. You could barely take care of yourself, much less an infant."

"But you could have done something to make sure my son was happy like you promised, not leave him in a home where the people didn't love him."

"He was a bastard child," Link snarled. "He got what he deserved."

Margaret's face blanched. "That's cruel and untrue. He didn't ask to be born."

Link growled. "I wish to hell you'd had the abortion like I suggested."

Margaret wiped at a tear. "I could never have done that, and you know it."

"I gave him a mother and father, and that was

enough," Link said, his voice tight. "It was better for all of us not to look back. Not to keep in touch. And my biggest mistake was that I didn't send him overseas to live with strangers instead of with the Kellers."

"Why them?" she asked.

"They'd lost a son and wanted a replacement. At the time, I thought it was best."

Taylor sighed. But the family obviously hadn't connected with Hayes.

"No." Margaret ran a hand through her hair. "It wasn't better for my son. He should have had loving parents. And some of this." She gestured around the room. "All our money and he had nothing."

"He will never have our name or our money," Link said. "I've worked too hard to build my reputation and to keep yours untainted for you to ruin it now. Leave the past behind, marry Goldenrod and look toward your future."

A long silence ensued, anger and accusations stretching between them. "I can't do that, Father. I know where my son is. I know the name those people gave him." Her voice turned shrill, growing nearly hysteric. "His name is Ranger Hayes Keller. And he's in your house, Father. A house that should have been a home to him all these years."

Link circled his desk and gripped Margaret by the arms. "But he doesn't know that, and he doesn't have to. What purpose would it serve now, Margaret? You're marrying Devon. Don't spoil that by dragging some bastard kid into the picture."

"Stop calling him that," Margaret snapped. "He deserves the truth. And I'm going to tell him."

She spun around and headed to the door, then swung it open. Taylor rushed behind her, and Link followed, his heels pounding angrily on the floor. He grabbed Taylor by the shoulder and forced her to look at him.

"This is your fault, Taylor. Fix it, and keep Margaret quiet and away from that ranger, or you'll be sorry."

Chapter Twelve

"Take your hands off of Miss Landis," Hayes ordered in a menacing tone.

Link Hathaway cut his gaze toward Hayes, a mixture of cold bitterness and another emotion Hayes couldn't define in his gray eyes. Eyes that chewed Hayes up and spit him out as if he was a nasty rodent who had invaded his lavish, ostentatious house and his perfectly orchestrated life.

"I said, take your hands off of her." He took another deliberate step toward the pompous ass. "And don't threaten her again or you'll deal with me."

"This is between me and my daughter," Hathaway said sharply. "Stay out of it, Ranger Keller."

"You're wrong about that," Hayes said. "I'm working a murder investigation, Mr. Hathaway, so anything that involves Taylor is my business. And from where I'm standing, you just threatened her."

"Get out," Hathaway barked.

"Father, stop it," Margaret said. "Hayes has a right—"

"He has no right." Link shot a warning look toward Taylor. "Tell her, Taylor."

Margaret's words echoed in Hayes's ears. What did she mean, he had a right? He searched her face, and a dozen tumultuous feelings darkened the depths of her eyes.

Taylor folded her arms around her waist. His mind boomeranged between all the elements of the case, all the questions that needed answers, the pieces that didn't quite fit into the puzzle yet.

"Does this have to do with that P.I.'s report?"

A thick unwavering silence stretched across the room, then Hayes addressed Link. "Mr. Hathaway, you're aware that a P.I. named Morris was murdered last night and that someone shot at Taylor."

A muscle ticked in Hathaway's jaw. "Maybe Miss Landis was simply in the wrong place at the wrong time."

"This is the third attempt on her life." He whirled around toward Taylor. "You're obviously keeping something from me. If the P.I. discovered something on Sutton and the city council, or if someone's blackmailing you or Margaret, then I need to know the reason."

Margaret moved closer to Taylor, a low sigh escaping her. "Taylor, it's all right."

Hayes glared at Taylor, tired of all the secrets and lies. "Maybe you had something to do with the illegal bids, Taylor."

Hurt registered on Taylor's face. "I would never do that."

"Then stop lying and tell me what the hell is going on."

"Taylor has done nothing wrong," Margaret said, drawing his gaze back to her. "In fact, she's been covering for me, trying to protect me."

He narrowed his eyes. "Protect you from what?"

Link cleared his throat and reached for Margaret's arm but she jerked away, fury flaring in her eyes. "No, Father. I'm going to tell him the truth. He deserves to know." Her voice cracked. "Besides, this man Morris might have been killed because of what he uncovered."

Hayes made a low sound in his throat. "Go on."

Margaret wet her lips with her tongue, and Taylor inched closer to her, placing a supportive hand on her back.

"When I was fifteen years old, I gave birth to a baby out of wedlock," Margaret said in a strained voice. "I gave that baby up for adoption, but I've always regretted it and wanted to know where my son was, if he was safe and happy." She hesitated, clenching her hands together, then brought them to her neck, twisting at a silver chain around her neck. "Taylor hired Mr. Morris to locate my child."

Hayes scowled. "And he did?"

She nodded, her face etched in pain.

"You think this is why Morris was killed?" Hayes asked.

She shrugged. "I don't know. I'm sure my case wasn't the only one he was working on."

"But it's possible," Hayes said. Rich people covering up their secrets.

"Stop this now." Hathaway reached for Margaret again, but she spun on him, planting her fisted hands on her hips. "No, Father, you lied to me, told me my son was happy, that he had a good life, but that wasn't true."

Hayes's chest began to throb, some germ of a thought sprouting as he began to connect the dots. Hathaway said he didn't belong here...Margaret had argued that he did...

He jerked his head toward Taylor, saw emotions darken her eyes, then Margaret's where tears began to trickle down her cheek.

"I'm so sorry, Hayes. I…"

"What are you saying?" Hayes asked through gritted teeth.

Margaret cleared her throat. "You're my son, the baby I gave up for adoption."

Shock rooted him to the spot, anger and humiliation and old feelings of abandonment clawing at him. "I don't believe you."

"It's true," Margaret said softly. "The papers were in that file Taylor gave me at lunch." She pushed them toward him, and Hayes took the papers and studied them, his jaw clenched.

He looked at Taylor for confirmation, and she nodded, sympathy in her eyes. He didn't want her damn pity.

Margaret reached for him. "I'm so sorry, Hayes—"

He cut her off. "You're sorry I'm that child?"

"No…" She shook her head and moved toward him again, extending her hand, her fingers sparkling with rubies.

Hayes held his callused one up to ward off her attempt to touch him. "Sorry I didn't turn out like you thought."

"Hayes, listen," Taylor whispered. "Margaret wanted to find you. She cares about you."

He shot Taylor a glacier look. Through the years, he'd imagined a million different reasons his mother might have given him up.

Because she was ill. Dying. Had no means to raise a child on her own. No family to support her. That she was killed by a vicious murderer. Or that he'd been stolen and that he had a family somewhere wondering where he was, waiting to reconcile with their kidnapped baby and bring him home.

But never had he dreamt that a spoiled heiress and her rich father had gotten rid of him because he would have interfered with their social schedule and prestigious lifestyle. "Yeah, she cared so much she abandoned me." He narrowed his eyes, accusing. "And you knew about this, Taylor. That's why you lied to me." His voice thickened and he worked to swallow the rage and pain clogging his throat. "You knew I was *her* son? The baby she threw away like trash."

"I didn't know until last night, when that private investigator called," Taylor whispered. "But I had to talk to Margaret first."

"Please understand, Hayes," Margaret cried. "I was only fifteen…a kid myself. Father thought it would be better, that you'd have two parents, a loving home—"

"A loving home?" A sarcastic chuckle escaped Hayes, echoing shrilly through the grand two-story foyer and bouncing off the elegant walls. Slowly the realization was sinking in. Link Hathaway was his grandfather. Had said he didn't belong.

And he was right. "My home was anything but loving." He gestured toward the ornate crystal chandelier, the original oil paintings, the vases that had probably cost more than a year's paycheck. "And nothing like this."

"I know that now," Margaret whispered. "But I didn't know back then. If I had, I would have done something sooner." She twisted the necklace, pulling a locket from beneath the shimmery fabric of her silk blouse and flipping it open. "See, this is a picture of you when you were born. I always wear it."

Another bitter laugh rolled from deep in his chest. "Right. Because you thought of me every day when you were hobnobbing with your rich friends."

"I did," Margaret cried. "I missed seeing you grow up and wondered what you were doing. And every year on your birthday I mourned for you, imagined what you looked like, how you'd changed, if you had a birthday party."

"I told you this was a mistake," Link Hathaway interjected.

It all came together in Hayes's mind, why Hathaway hadn't wanted her to tell him. He wanted to protect what was his. His money, his wealth, his power and image.

"Well, there weren't any parties," Hayes said dryly. "But I understand how you wouldn't want a kid messing up your rich snotty lifestyle or your social calendar." He directed a condescending look toward Hathaway, hating the man. "You people don't care about anything but your wealth and how you look. But don't worry. I don't want your damn money."

"Hayes, please, listen…" Margaret pleaded.

Hayes's fists tightened. "Just answer me one question. Who is my father?"

Margaret gulped. "I'm sorry, but I can't tell you that."

"Can't or won't?" Hayes barked.

"I can't," Margaret said in a choked whisper. "He doesn't know about you. He was young, too… I never told him I was pregnant."

Hayes felt sucker punched. His heart pounding, he

spun around and rushed outside. He had to escape these people, wished he'd never come to Cantara Hills.

Wished he didn't know the truth and had never met the woman who'd given birth to him and hadn't wanted him.

TAYLOR'S HEART ACHED for Margaret and for Hayes. She turned to fold Margaret in her arms, but Margaret shook her head. "Go after him, Taylor. Please…make sure he's all right. He needs someone right now."

The pain and desolation in her friend's eyes tore at her, but Margaret was right. The best thing she could do for her was to comfort Hayes. To convince him that Margaret loved him. That they could have a relationship now.

If only he'd give her the chance.

"You'll be all right?"

Margaret nodded and gently coaxed her toward the door. "Please, he shouldn't be alone."

Not that he'd want her with him, but Taylor nodded and rushed outside anyway. Hayes was sitting in his SUV, the engine sputtering to life, anger emanating from his icy glare as she settled in the passenger side.

"Why don't you stay here with your rich friends?"

"Don't be a snob, Hayes," Taylor said.

His eyes darkened, a muscle ticking in his jaw. "You took me along today to watch the two of you try on those damn dresses, and you knew all along and didn't tell me."

His accusation stung. "I wanted to, Hayes, but it wasn't my secret to share."

Walt Caldwell, Link Hathaway's chauffeur, drove up then and climbed out. Taylor glanced up and noticed his uniform. Her breath caught as the shiny brass button on Walt's uniform flickered in the sunlight. Hayes was studying it, too.

No… It was a perfect match.

"Who else was aware you'd hired that private investigator?" Hayes asked.

"No one that I know of," Taylor said.

His shoulders stiffened, but pain edged his voice. "Who else knew about me?"

She glanced at the Hathaway mansion. "Just Margaret's father…I think." She reached for his hand, covered it with her own. "He told Margaret that he'd checked on you over the years, that you were healthy and happy and in a good home, Hayes. Margaret… loved you. You have to believe that, to try and understand the circumstances—"

"I understand perfectly." Hayes jerked his hand from hers, then spun from the driveway and onto the main road. "But your case just took on a new list of suspects, Taylor. Hathaway obviously didn't want Margaret to find me, and if he discovered you'd hired a private investigator, he would have tried to bury the search. I'm going to have to question him about that but I'll get a warrant first."

Taylor winced and buckled her seat belt as Hayes pushed the gas and accelerated. But his words haunted her.

Link certainly would do anything to protect his daughter. He'd lied to Margaret to prevent her from looking for her child.

Had he discovered the P.I. was searching for Hayes, and killed Morris to keep the truth about Hayes quiet? She gripped the seat edge as Hayes took a turn too fast. Had Link tried to kill her to keep her from finding Margaret's son?

Hayes cursed as he checked the rearview mirror, then increased his speed. "Hold on, we've got a tail."

She glanced over her shoulder and saw a dark sedan with tinted windows speeding up their rear. Tires screeched as they careened around a curve, then a shot pinged off the back glass, shattering the window.

Chapter Thirteen

"Hellfire and damnation!" Hayes swerved, tires screeching as another bullet bounced through the car and grazed the seat. The SUV skidded toward a stop sign, sliding through and barely managing to miss an Expedition flying the other way. The driver honked madly, and Hayes checked the rearview mirror to get a look at the shooter, but the windows were so dark that he couldn't distinguish a face. Then the sedan spun off on a side street and headed the other way.

"Taylor, are you okay?"

She'd ducked in the seat and covered her head with her hands. "Yes. Are you?"

"Yeah, but I'd like to choke that son of a bitch in the sedan."

"Is he gone?"

"It looks that way."

He turned into Cantara Hills, then on to the street to Taylor's estate. She uncovered her head and sat up, eyes wide with fear. Adrenaline had flooded his system, and he had to force himself to ease up on the gas and slow down.

"Did you see him?" Taylor asked.

"No, the windows were tinted too dark." He pulled up to the gate and slid the key card into the slot, then drove up the winding drive to her garage. Sweat had beaded on his neck and forehead, and he wiped it away, grateful at the moment to be at Taylor's mansion with closed gates.

At least she'd be temporarily safe.

They both climbed out, the silence a deafening roar charged with questions and the tension from the past hour.

He verified that the security system was on, then allowed Taylor to unlock the door and punch in the code.

"I need to bag these bullet casings and send them to forensics."

She nodded. "Is there anything I can do, Hayes?"

Her question was loaded with innuendo, with a reference to the fact that he'd just learned Margaret Hathaway was his mother. But Hayes couldn't deal with that now, not with her. He felt too raw, too…exposed.

"No. I'm going to call Brody and Egan so we can discuss the investigation."

"I'm sorry, Hayes. For everything."

The sincerity in her voice tugged at his heart, one he'd guarded for too long. One he couldn't open to her now, especially with her close friendship to the woman who'd given birth to him then tossed him away.

"You realize that the man who rummaged through your office the night he tried to strangle you in the pool might have been looking for the information from Morris."

Her eyes flickered with distress. "I suppose it's possible."

"When did you hire him? Before the car bomb?"

Her face paled and she nodded. "But I didn't tell anyone."

Hayes frowned. "If Morris was poking around, Hathaway could have heard about it. And judging from his reaction, he might have hired someone to find that report."

Pain darkened her eyes. "Hayes, I know he was tough tonight, but I don't really think he'd hire someone to kill me."

Hayes arched a brow. "Why not, Taylor? He'd do anything to protect his wealth, his daughter and his social standing. And your search threatened all of that."

"He only wanted to protect Margaret, Hayes. She was so young when she had you—"

He jerked his hand up, cutting off any further discussion. "Please, spare me, Taylor. I know how you rich people think."

Anger reddened Taylor's face. "You are such a snob, Hayes. I understand you're hurting now and that you received a bum rap, but if you'd knock that chip off your shoulder for a second, you'd see that not everyone who has money is evil." Her ragged breath pierced the air. "Margaret is kind and loving and has felt guilty about giving you up for years. Why do you think she never married? She didn't think she deserved happiness because she regretted giving up her child."

"I've seen her picture in the society pages," Hayes snapped. "She didn't look so miserable to me."

"She tried to make a life," Taylor argued. "But she thought about you every day, she told me that. She even funds a teen center for pregnant girls to offer them counseling because she never received any when she needed it most. Only pressure from her father to give you up for adoption and his assurance that you'd be better off."

"Right." His voice dripped sarcasm. "The truth was that Link Hathaway was better off without a bastard child ruining his life. But don't worry, Taylor, I don't intend to ask him or Margaret for anything." His chest ached from the pressure of not shouting at her.

Memories of their heated interlude the night before rose to taunt him. She'd known the truth then. "Is that why you kissed me, why you came on to me, Taylor? Because you felt sorry for me and wanted to soften the blow for your friend, hoping I'd understand and not make trouble?"

Hurt and anger reared in her eyes, and she reached back and slapped him. "I can't believe you'd suggest such a thing. You can be a bastard, Hayes."

His jaw stung. "Yes, well, that I am."

Taylor sighed. "Oh, God…I'm sorry. I didn't mean it like that, Hayes."

He spoke through clenched teeth. "I don't want pity sex because you feel sorry for me."

Her lip quivered, a dozen emotions flaring in her eyes. Hurt. Anger. Sympathy. Compassion. Desire.

She wet her lips, then reached up and cupped his face with her hands. "I didn't kiss you out of pity," she whispered. "And you know that, Hayes."

She dragged him toward her, fusing her mouth with his.

Pure hunger and raw primal need raced through his blood, obliterating his fury and erasing common sense. He wanted to forget the case. Forget that she'd kept secrets from him and made him feel inadequate and vulnerable. That she was best friends with his birth mother, the woman he'd tried so hard to forget all his life.

That she'd seen him endure one of the most painful moments of his life.

A maelstrom of emotions clogged his throat, but she ran her hands along his jaw, scraping rough beard stubble, and moaning as she plunged her tongue inside his mouth.

He sucked it in, drawing in the essence of her sensuality as he tasted the passion seeping through her pores and flaming his body with a need so strong that he clutched her to him and deepened the kiss. She stroked his shoulders, then lowered her hands to claw at his back.

His body hardened, his sex throbbing and aching for fulfillment, for her. But reality gnawed at him, chopping away at his hunger and rekindling the pain raging below the surface of that unbidden lust.

He ordered himself to pull away, but she tore her mouth from his, her eyes hooded and molten hot with hunger and the unbridled passion that steeped below the surface. Her ragged breathing echoed in the tense silence between them.

"Did that feel like pity to you, Hayes?"

She squared her shoulders, a dare glinting in her eyes.

No, it didn't. But the passion between them was strictly physical. Stemmed from the danger confronting her and the adrenaline from their earlier attack.

When things returned to normal, she would write him off and go back to her rich men.

But he'd remember that for a moment he'd had a beautiful heiress in his arms. And he'd be haunted by the fact that he'd just met his mother.

Hell, he was a Texas Ranger. He couldn't forget that he was here to protect her.

And that the reason someone had tried to kill her might be because of him. Because she'd hired a P.I. to find Margaret's son. That his own grandfather wished he would go away and blamed Taylor for screwing things up.

"Did it, Hayes?"

He steeled himself against the blatant hunger threatening to rob him of his sanity.

"It doesn't matter what it is," he said coldly. "I'm here to do a job. To find out who's trying to kill you." He took another step back, knowing if he didn't, he'd cave and drag her back into his arms. He possessed only so much resistance, and she was hacking at it with a sharp knife.

"You almost died three times, Taylor. And now I know it might be because of me."

Her soft gasp filled the air. "Hayes…no, it's not your fault."

He clenched his jaw. "I'm going to find who's targeted you, Taylor. Then I'll leave Cantara Hills, and you and Margaret and Link Hathaway will never have to worry about me bothering you again." His voice held a razor-sharp, firm edge, yet feelings for her simmered beneath the edge of his calm. Feelings he didn't welcome but was helpless to stop.

As much as he didn't want to admit it, he admired her loyalty to her friends, the fact that she'd faced his wrath because she'd respected Margaret's right to tell him the truth. That she even fought to convince him that Margaret really cared.

And when that SOB had shot at them earlier, all he had

thought about was protecting Taylor, not letting any harm come to her because he couldn't stand to see her in pain.

Or dead.

"Hayes—"

"Shh." He raked his gaze over her, knowing that if he didn't leave her this second, he'd do something stupid, like make love to her.

Or fall for her and lose his heart.

So he simply stroked her hair behind her ear. "I promised to keep you safe, and I will. And if Hathaway tried to kill you or hired someone to do his dirty work, I will put the SOB behind bars, even if he is my grandfather."

Barely holding on to his ironclad control, he retreated to the guest room to sort out the clues to the case. First he had to call Egan and inform him of what he'd learned. That now they had additional suspects.

That a button from his father's uniform had been found at the scene of a murder investigation. An investigation that now led back to Egan's father's boss.

That Walt was now at the top of their list of suspects because he would do anything for Link Hathaway, was loyal to him to a fault.

God…how had things gotten so screwed up?

Egan and his father had never been close. In fact, Walt had been cold to Egan. But how would Egan feel when he found out that his father might be the killer they were working their asses off to find?

TAYLOR'S BODY TINGLED with need as she retreated to her office. Never had a man gotten her so tied up in knots. One minute she wanted to slap Hayes out of his ever-loving mind, and the next she wanted to take him to her bedroom and make love for hours. Maybe days.

He was so darn stubborn.

So sure that her money was a barrier between them when it didn't have to be that way. Love was all that mattered....

Love? Good grief, she couldn't be falling in love with Hayes Keller.

Not Margaret's son, a man who had too much pride for his own good. Would that pride prevent him from forgiving Margaret?

And what about Margaret's father?

Had Link Hathaway tried to have her killed because she'd nosed into his business? God...if so, Margaret would be devastated.

Why was all this happening, especially right before Margaret's wedding, when she was finally going to be happy?

She pinched the bridge of her nose, her head throbbing from tension. Knowing she'd go crazy if she didn't keep busy, she accessed her computer files to finalize the plans for the party she was giving to honor Margaret's engagement.

She flipped on the small television in the corner and listened to the news while she worked, a news clip catching her eye. Kenneth Sutton onstage, giving a speech about his political views and plans for the state when he was elected governor. Tammy, dressed immaculately in a linen designer summer dress, smiled behind him, the perfect politician's wife. The camera panned sideways and landed on Devon Goldenrod, Margaret's fiancé. Devon's sandy-blond hair and

Armani suit showcased his handsome face and athletic build, but something about his smile seemed forced.

He had always been second to Kenneth Sutton, second in the city council election four years earlier. Second in the class where the two men had graduated together.

Hmm…had Devon minded?

She shook off the thought. Now that Kenneth was running for governor, Devon was a shoe-in for the city council.

So who would want to make Kenneth look bad or frame him for the illegal bids? She dug through the files again searching for answers.

Anything to distract herself from Hayes in the other room and to keep from going to him.

HAYES HAD SET UP THE SITTING room that adjoined the guest bedroom suite as an office with a whiteboard for notes and a corkboard where he tacked photos of each of the suspects in the case and the crimes and arrests leading up to Taylor's attack. Montoya, who had killed Kimberly McQuade. Carlson Woodward who had tried to kill Caroline Stallings.

And his main suspects. Miles Landis. Kenneth Sutton. Tammy Sutton. Now he needed to add Link Hathaway and Walt Caldwell. But he had to talk to Egan first. He owed his friend a heads-up.

He phoned Egan and asked him to get Brody and meet him at the estate. While he waited he reviewed the case from the beginning, trying to piece it all together.

Wet shoe prints had been found on Caroline's floor during the break-in and attempt on Caroline's life, but forensics hadn't determined the source. The print belonged to a size eleven but anyone could have worn them to conceal his real foot size. The Rangers believed those shoes belonged to Miles because they'd seen them on the surveillance video footage and seen a pair in Miles's gym bag. Of course, someone could have stolen them.

The explosive devices in Caroline's garage and Taylor's car were set on timers and were low-tech, meaning they didn't require a skilled person to make them. With the Internet, any of their suspects could have found directions and followed them.

The house key that Caroline had given Tammy and Kenneth was still missing. And the toxicology report on Carlson Woodward proved that he'd been drugged. The drugs could have triggered his violent behavior and spurred him to try to kill Caroline.

The question was—had he voluntarily taken the drugs or had someone else drugged him?

Someone who was now trying to kill Taylor?

Although Taylor claimed no one else knew about the private investigator's search for Margaret's son—him—so that wouldn't have been their motive.

On to the more recent facts. The hair he'd found the night of the pool attack on Taylor belonged to Tammy Sutton and proved she'd been at Taylor's, but it could have been left at any time.

The button from Morris's office belonged to Walt Caldwell who they had to question.

The bullet casings from the private investigator's office, and the bullet casings from his SUV had both come from a .38. But where was the gun?

Several prints had been found at the private investigator's office, including Taylor's but not Link's or

Walt's. And two others that weren't in the system but might be useful later if they needed to match them with an arrest.

The buzzer for security chirped, and he answered it, then let Egan and Brody in. A frown marred Brody's face as he strode into the room.

The tension was only going to get thicker, Hayes thought. Especially between him and Egan.

Egan jammed his hands in his jeans pockets and leaned against the wall. "You got a lead on Taylor's attacker?"

He shrugged. "Maybe. There's definitely been a new development."

Brody crossed his arms. "Spill it, Keller."

Hayes took a deep breath. "I found out the reason Taylor went to meet that private investigator and maybe the motive for his murder."

"Good work," Egan said. "Fill us in."

Hayes cleared the cobwebs from his throat. "Margaret Hathaway had a baby when she was fifteen, but gave the baby up for adoption. Taylor hired Morris to find out where the child was." He hesitated. "And he did."

"You think that's what got him killed?" Brody asked.

"It's looking that way." He dragged in a breath. "It also turns out that that kid was me."

Brody's eyes shot up and Egan's mouth opened and closed. "Margaret Hathaway is your mother?" Brody croaked.

Hayes swallowed hard and nodded.

"You saw proof?" Egan asked.

Hayes nodded again. "Yep. Saw the birth certificate and adoption papers where my mama signed me away."

"Holy hell, Hayes," Egan said. "That means your family is rich."

"Yeah, rich." He grunted in disgust. "But I don't want their damn money. And Link Hathaway made it plain and clear that I'd have no part in their happy little family."

"What about Margaret?" Brody asked quietly.

A sharp pain twisted his insides. "I don't want to talk about it." He cleared his throat, forcing a calm veneer to his voice. "Anyway, the point is that Link calculated to keep my existence a secret. He didn't want Margaret locating her child."

"Which would give him a motive for murdering the private investigator," Egan said, jumping on his train of thought.

"And Taylor," Hayes added. "I overheard him tell her that it was her fault, and that she would be sorry for nosing into his business."

Brody whistled, and Hayes tacked Hathaway's picture onto the corkboard, then pointed to the picture of the button. "I found this button at the private investigator's office beside his body."

He waited, watched, saw the moment Egan recognized the button. His gaze swung to Hayes's, questions exploding in his eyes.

"You know who that belongs to?" Tension strained Egan's voice.

Hayes nodded.

Disbelief, then pain and worry flashed in Egan's eyes. "And you think my father killed Morris for Link Hathaway."

Chapter Fourteen

Hayes lifted his shoulders in a shrug. "I don't know," he said honestly. "But we have to question him and Hathaway."

"What about your father?" Egan asked in a low voice. "Maybe he didn't want Taylor snooping around. And maybe he didn't want you found, either."

Egan's comment cut to the bone. "That's possible." He ground out the words. "But Margaret claims he doesn't know I exist. She never told him she was pregnant."

"He could have found out," Egan pointed out.

Hayes couldn't argue that point. Meaning Hayes's father would be a suspect, as well.

Egan phoned Walt and requested they meet at his old house but offered no explanation.

"I'll call for a warrant for Link Hathaway's house and Walt's," Brody said.

"Remember we're looking for a .38, probably unregistered." Hayes gestured toward the photos on the corkboard and the whiteboard information. "In our preliminary research, I discovered that Hathaway has a .45 and a .38, Tammy Sutton a .22 and Kenneth owns a .38." He turned to Egan. "Does your father own a gun?"

Egan shook his head. "Not that I know of."

But he could have bought one without Egan knowing.

Egan clapped his hands together. "I say we pick up that warrant, then get this over with."

"I'll work on obtaining Hathaway's phone records while you're gone," Brody said.

Hayes grimaced. Recently Walt had called Egan and apologized for giving him such a crappy childhood. Egan hadn't totally forgiven him but they'd started to mend their relationship.

This would throw a kink in that reconciliation.

Hayes caught Egan's arm. "Listen, man, I'm sorry."

Egan stared him in the eyes, his jaw tight. "Yeah, so am I."

Hayes nodded. Neither of them had expected this investigation to be turned on its tail and implicate their own family members.

But now they had, they had to follow through. After all, they were Texas Rangers and the badge required it.

THE PAIN IN HAYES'S EYES roused emotions and protective instincts that Taylor had never felt for a man.

Yet she also felt protective over Margaret, and knew her friend was in turmoil, too. Besides, Hayes was wrong. Margaret had missed him, had seen his face in every child she'd tried to help since.

She didn't simply donate money to charities. She spent time at the teen center, had even earned a counseling degree and counseled girls on teen pregnancy.

A knock sounded on the door. "Come in."

She expected to see Hayes's face, but Ranger McQuade appeared instead. "Miss Landis, I just wanted to let you know that I'll be downstairs filling in for Hayes for a while. He and Egan went to question Link Hathaway and Walt Caldwell."

She nodded and picked up the phone as he closed the door. So that was the way Hayes wanted to play it. He'd leave his friend to babysit her so he could interrogate Margaret's father.

She had to warn Margaret.

She punched in the number for Margaret's cell phone, hoping to avoid Link and speak directly to her friend. Margaret answered on the third ring, her voice hoarse.

"Margaret, are you all right?"

Margaret sniffled. "I don't know, Taylor. Part of me wants to jump for joy that I finally found my son. But he hates me, and I don't know how to make it up to him for all that he lost."

Taylor winced. "He doesn't hate you," she said gently. "He's just bitter right now, and in shock."

"I never meant to hurt him," Margaret said in earnest. "I did think Daddy was right at the time."

"And if the people who took Hayes in had loved him, he probably would have been. You were only a kid yourself and needed to finish school, Margaret."

"But he'll never forgive me," Margaret said. "And I want to have a relationship with him."

"Give him time," Taylor advised. "You both need that, Margaret." Maybe Hayes would come around at the party Saturday night.

"I suppose you're right." A long pause ensued. "But I have to tell Devon. Maybe postpone the wedding."

"Margaret, do you think that's necessary?" Taylor clawed her hand through her hair. It had taken Margaret months to agree to marry Devon. She hated for her to postpone it any longer.

Devon would understand. Wouldn't he?

Or would it affect his run for the city council if Margaret's illegitimate child were revealed?

"How are things between you and your father?" Taylor asked.

"Tense," Margaret said. "He encouraged me to let Hayes go without even trying to get to know him, but I can't do that. I won't."

Relief surged through Taylor at the conviction in her friend's voice. Link had manipulated Margaret far too long. He needed to see that forging a relationship with her son would finally fill the void in Margaret's life.

"Speaking of your father and Hayes," Taylor said. "I think he's on his way over there to talk to him now."

Margaret's soft gasp echoed over the line. "About me?"

A ripple of panic darted through Taylor. "About that private investigator's murder."

"Oh my Lord," Margaret rasped. "Hayes thinks that my father killed Mr. Morris because he didn't want me to find out about him."

Unable to verbally answer that question, she let the silence serve as her reply.

"He's wrong," Margaret insisted. "My father would never hurt anyone, Taylor."

Again, Taylor couldn't respond. She hoped Margaret

was right, but Link had never intended for his secrets about Hayes to be revealed. He probably feared that if Margaret discovered his lies, he'd lose his daughter.

EGAN INSISTED ON DRIVING, and Hayes agreed. The silence between them was deafening as they parked at Egan's father's house, a modest home in the same neighborhood where he, Egan and Brody had grown up and connected as kids. Three boys who'd liked rough-housing, sports and fighting, who'd been like brothers.

Now this case might tear them apart.

He followed Egan up the overgrown sidewalk, wondering why Walt didn't take more pride in his own place and why he was so ridiculously dedicated to Link Hathaway. Obviously not because he earned an exorbitant salary or had been given a fancy car.

Not like the limousine Walt drove for Link.

As kids, the boys had begged Egan's father to take them for a ride in the swanky black vehicle, but Link had refused Walt the privilege, saying the car was too nice for hooligans like them.

They had all despised Link Hathaway.

And now that Hayes knew the man was his grandfather, he hated him even more.

Although this house had once been Egan's home, Egan balled his hand into a fist and pounded on the door, alerting his father to the fact that he had stopped by.

"Dad, it's Egan. We have to talk."

Walt approached from the back bedroom, looking disheveled. "What in God's name is going on?" Walt bellowed. "I need to be at work, Egan."

Egan shoved the search warrant into his father's hands. "Dad, this is official. We have a warrant to search your house and car."

Walt's shocked gaze swung to Egan, then Hayes. "You've got to be kidding."

Egan chewed the inside of his cheek. "I'm afraid not. One of the buttons off your uniform was found at the scene of a murder investigation, Dad."

Walt sucked air between his teeth. "How do you know it's mine?"

"It's identical to the one on your uniform," Hayes said, cutting in. "And we matched your prints, as well."

Walt sighed shakily and sank into his big plaid recliner. "I can explain."

"Yeah?" Egan snapped. "I bet you can."

"Don't disrespect me, son," Walt snarled.

Hayes cleared his throat. "We have to follow every lead. Can you explain your relationship to a P.I. named Mr. Morris?"

"Morris?"

"Yes."

Walt cut his steely blue-gray eyes sideways, shifting restlessly. "I don't have a relationship with the man."

"Look, Dad, there's no need to lie or deny that you knew him," Egan said in a clipped tone. "We have prints proving that you were in his office. And Morris is dead."

"I did go there," Walt admitted. "But he was already dead when I arrived."

"What was the nature of your visit?" Hayes asked.

"I'm not at liberty to say," Walt said.

"You work for Link Hathaway," Hayes accused. "You went there for him, didn't you? You knew that his daughter had a baby when she was a teenager and gave it up for adoption?"

Walt's eyes widened. "How did you find that out? No one was supposed to know."

Hayes's jaw tightened. "You obviously did. Did you help Link get rid of the kid when he was born?"

Walt's face turned a pasty greenish white, and Hayes's stomach clenched. "You did, didn't you?"

Walt gripped the chair edge. "I was his driver. I did what he told me to do."

The picture of the events of that night rolled through Hayes's mind in a sickening drunken rush. Margaret giving birth. Link sending Walt off to dispose of the child.

To dispose of him.

"Link discovered that Taylor Landis had hired Morris to find Margaret's child," Egan said, his tone hard, yet pain darkened his eyes. "And he sent you to take care of his business, didn't he, Dad?"

Walt lurched to his feet. "I went there, yes, but I didn't kill Morris. He was already dead when I arrived."

Hayes arched a brow. "Really?"

"I swear it." Walt turned a panicked look toward Egan. "Honest, son, I smelled blood the minute I walked in, and stooped down to see if the man was alive." His hand combed over his uniform finding the missing button. "That's when I must have lost the button. He didn't have a pulse, and I heard a sound and thought the killer might still be there, so I ran as fast as I could."

"You didn't call 9-1-1?" Hayes accused.

Walt swiped a hand over his sweating face. "I…was going to, but then sirens wailed and I figured someone else heard the shots and had called it in."

"And you didn't want to stick around and answer questions?" Egan asked.

"I...didn't want to expose my reason for being there. Link Hathaway's interests had to be protected."

"What about yours?" Egan asked.

Walt reached for Egan, but Egan snapped a hand back. "Stop it, Dad. I don't know why you're so dedicated to that man."

Walt glanced back and forth between the two of them. "He's not a bad man. He only wanted to protect his daughter."

"Do you have a gun in the house?" Egan asked.

Walt shook his head. "No, you know I don't like guns, Egan."

"I have to look anyway, Dad." He paused. "You know that if you're covering for Link Hathaway or lying, you can be charged as an accomplice to murder."

"I didn't kill anyone, son," Walt said firmly.

But he still might be covering for Hathaway. Egan stared at his father for a long moment, then strode toward the hall desk and started to search.

Hayes gritted his teeth. "Answer me one more question, Walt. Did you know that I was Margaret's son, the one Hathaway threw away?"

Walt staggered backward, then slumped into the chair again. "No, I had no idea. All Link said was that he told Margaret the kid was happy."

So that part of Margaret's story was true. But it didn't mean that his grandfather wasn't a killer.

"What about my father?" Hayes's throat felt dry as if he had sawdust clogging it. "Do you know his name?"

Walt gave him a steady look. "Mr. Hathaway never

told me his name, and I never asked. Didn't think it was any of my business."

But it was *his* business, and his father might be the killer.

Chapter Fifteen

By the time they reached Cantara Hills, Hayes had adopted his poker face. He refused to allow Hathaway to know how much he was hurting. On some level, he realized Margaret had only been a kid herself and under the direction of an overbearing powerful father when she'd given him up.

Keeping him would have ruined her life.

But the ache of being unwanted ate at him, especially knowing Hathaway had had the money to give him a decent home.

His gut tightened as Egan parked in front of the mansion. Margaret's pricey car still sat in the enormous garage.

Egan whistled. "I still can't get used to walking up to these damn estates." He eyed Hayes. "Unbelievable, man, that your mother grew up here."

Hayes growled. "I can't think of Margaret Hathaway like that."

"They owe you," Egan said in a low voice.

"I don't want anything from them but the truth." And to know if Hathaway had tried to kill Taylor.

He focused on that thought as he and Egan crossed the path to the front door and knocked. A minute later, a butler answered the door.

Egan cut straight to the point. "We need to speak to Mr. Hathaway. And we have a search warrant for the premises."

The butler's expression was stony, but he led them to Hathaway's office. "I'll call Mr. Hathaway."

Egan and Hayes both nodded, Hayes's gaze traveling around the glitzy interior again and landing on a portrait of Margaret hanging over the fireplace. She wore a graduation cap and gown, so it must have been in high school, probably a finishing school. If she had been fifteen when he was born, this picture was taken afterward. He stepped closer, studying her youthful face, yet something about her eyes disturbed him. They held a haunting sadness that made his throat thicken.

Had she regretted giving up custody of him? Had she missed him and thought of him over the years?

Was it possible that she really cared about him?

The sound of Hathaway clearing his throat jerked him back to the present. "What are you doing back here?"

Hayes gritted his teeth. "We have a search warrant."

"You can't think that I killed that private investigator?" Hathaway barked. "Unlike you, I'm a prominent well-respected citizen of this community."

Unlike him. The words echoed through his head, rousing his temper.

"Father, don't speak to him like that." Margaret moved into the arched doorway, her frame elegant and graceful, although wariness filled her eyes.

Hathaway pivoted, his jaw set. "He practically accused me of murder. Now he knows who he is, he wants to get revenge on us. Hell, he's probably going to plant a gun to frame me so he can go after my money."

Margaret's eyes flared with anger. "Stop it, Father. He's not here to do any such thing." She gave Hayes an odd look, a mixture of hurt that he'd accuse her father of a crime and acceptance that he had to ask questions. "Hayes, is this really necessary?"

Egan cleared his throat. "Yes, ma'am. We have to check out every lead. And right now, your father is a prime suspect in Mr. Morris's murder." His voice turned low. "We also questioned my own father and searched his house."

He didn't have to add that explanation, but Hayes realized that Egan was smoothing things for him.

Hayes wasn't ready to latch on to the olive branch.

Hathaway reached for the phone. "I'm going to call my attorney. Don't say anything else, Margaret."

"I need you to tell me my father's name," Hayes said.

Margaret winced. "I told you he has nothing to do with this, Hayes. He really doesn't know about you."

"But he could have found out, so you have to tell me."

She hesitated, tears blurring her eyes. "All right. But please let me talk to him first. He has a right to hear that he has a son from me."

He hesitated, considered what she was asking. If his father really didn't know, then he deserved the truth from Margaret. But allowing her to tell him might put her in danger.

Her eyes were so pleading, though, that he relented. "All right. But do it soon."

She nodded, the anguish in her eyes tearing at him.

Still, if she was wrong, his father could have offed Morris to keep Hayes from finding the truth.

Link Hathaway could have done the same thing.

"Mr. Hathaway, you keep a gun here?" he asked.

A vein bulged in Hathaway's forehead but he nodded.

"Would you get it, please?" Egan said.

Hathaway reached inside the cherry credenza, retrieved a key and unlocked the top desk drawer. "Holy hell," he muttered.

"What is it?" Margaret asked.

He jerked his head up, his gaze wide-eyed. "My .38 is missing."

Margaret gasped, and Hayes and Egan exchanged looks. Was Hathaway feigning surprise or had he known the gun was gone?

"You always keep it in that drawer, not a safe?" Egan asked.

"Yes."

Hayes narrowed his eyes. "When was the last time you saw it?"

Hathaway scratched his head. "A few days ago."

"Dad?" Margaret's voice sounded shaky.

"I haven't had any reason to get it," Hathaway said defensively.

Egan crossed his arms. "Who has had access to your office?"

Hathaway furrowed his brow in thought. "The staff…" He glanced at Egan. "Walt. But none of them would steal it."

"Are you sure? Any of them or another visitor might have seen where you keep the key," Egan pointed out.

"Who else has been here?" Hayes asked, unconvinced that Hathaway hadn't used it to kill Morris, then ditched it.

Hathaway glanced at Margaret and hesitated.

Margaret twisted the silver chain again, drawing Hayes's eyes toward the locket, the one holding his baby picture. "Dad, who?" Margaret whispered.

A long-suffering sigh escaped him. "Devon stopped by yesterday morning. And Kenneth and Tammy Sutton were here for lunch."

Hayes grimaced. Sutton once again. But another thought niggled at him. "Devon knows you had a child, Margaret?"

Panic blazed in her eyes. "Yes."

"He knew you were looking for him?"

Her expression turned wary. "I mentioned it to him."

"What was his reaction?" Egan asked.

She hesitated. "He thought I should leave the past in the past."

Hayes grunted. "If he knew Taylor had hired the P.I., he could have tried to stop him from giving her the information."

"But he didn't know that Taylor had hired Mr. Morris," Margaret argued.

"How did you know about Morris, Mr. Hathaway?" Hayes asked.

Hathaway shifted and jammed his hands in the pockets of his pleated designer suit. "The damn fool came to me and showed me the documents he'd found."

Hayes's suspicions rose. "And what did you do?"

Hathaway glanced at Margaret, his shoulders tensing. "I offered to pay him to keep quiet."

Bribery, Hayes thought sourly. "Did he accept your offer?"

Hathaway shook his head. "Said he had already been compensated. And he refused to tell me who hired him."

But Hathaway had somehow found out. Hayes would bet money on it.

And he might have told Goldenrod. Then Margaret's father and fiancé could have conspired to keep Taylor and Margaret from learning about him.

"I have to talk to Devon Goldenrod," Hayes said.

Margaret thumbed her hand through her hair. "He's out of town and won't be back until tomorrow right before the party at Taylor's."

"Party?"

Margaret winced. "Yes, Taylor insisted on throwing it in honor of the wedding."

A wedding he would have to attend as Taylor's bodyguard. A wedding where he'd watch his mother marry a man who had just been added to his list of murder suspects.

Chapter Sixteen

Taylor's stomach was so tied in knots, she found herself in the kitchen again. She made homemade pasta with fresh salmon, a spinach salad, appetizers of prosciutto and melon, garlic bread, and a decadent chocolate turtle pie.

She wondered if Hayes liked chocolate turtle pie. Or salmon.

And what was happening with him and Margaret and Link Hathaway.

Ranger McQuade was poring over Link's phone records in the living room when Hayes returned. Her stomach vaulted to her throat as he entered.

The other ranger was missing in action—had he gone back to Caroline?

At first, she'd thought Caroline crazy for falling for Egan Caldwell, but now she understood the earthy sensual magnetism of these rangers. They were real men. Down to earth, strong, gutsy, protective...masculine and sexy as hell.

Heaven help her, but he looked so damn tempting in that dark Stetson with his dark eyes so brooding. His permanent five o'clock shadow only added to his mysterious soulful look, and her hands itched to touch him.

Instead she placed the appetizers on the bar along with a bottle of red wine, Scotch and a beer mug, just in case she could convince Hayes to have a drink with her.

Or more…

She'd never actually tried to seduce a man, but her imagination had had a field day the past hour, and she'd fantasized about the two of them working their frustrations out in bed.

What would Margaret say if Taylor slept with her son?

If she knew that Taylor was starting to have feelings for him?

He glanced at the bar as he entered, an eyebrow arched at the display of food. "Expecting company?"

"Just you," she said, her cheeks heating.

An odd look simmered in his eyes…desire? Heat? Surprise?

Then he quickly masked it and grunted at Ranger McQuade when he loped in. "What's the scoop?" Brody asked.

Hayes frowned. "Walt Caldwell claims Morris was dead when he arrived. He didn't stick around because he heard a noise and thought the killer might still be there. We didn't find a gun at his place."

Brody harrumphed. "So he knew about you?"

"He claimed he didn't know my name," Hayes said. "Just that Hathaway was asking questions. He intended to bribe the P.I. to keep quiet, but was too late."

"How'd Egan take it?" Brody asked.

Hayes shook his head. "He didn't say much. But I think he believes his father."

"And Hathaway?" Brody asked.

Hayes glanced at Taylor, his expression hooded. "Hathaway has a .38 but it was conveniently missing. The staff, Margaret's fiancé, Devon Goldenrod, Egan's father and the Suttons all had access to his office."

Brody leaned one palm against the granite bar. "The suspects keep piling up."

"Yeah," Hayes agreed. "We stopped by Sutton's after we left Hathaway's, and he offered his weapon. I checked it and it hasn't been fired recently. No GSR on his hands, either."

"So Sutton didn't shoot Morris?"

"Could have hired someone," Hayes suggested.

"True. What else did Hathaway say?"

Hayes blew out a breath. "Link Hathaway admits he knew Morris was looking for Margaret's child, but Morris refused the bribe."

"A P.I. with morals," Brody muttered. "That's original."

Hayes's mouth almost twitched with a smile, and something tickled inside Taylor's belly. She wanted to see him smile, see him happy.

Good grief. What was wrong with her? She poured herself a glass of wine then gestured in offering, but Brody shook his head and Hayes declined, as well, mumbling that he was on duty.

Yeah, being her bodyguard.

She wanted his body instead.

"Another twist, though," Hayes said. "Apparently Devon Goldenrod knows that Margaret had a baby and didn't want her looking for the kid."

Taylor's lungs tightened. Hayes uttered the comment as if he was a distant observer and this was just a case, not his mother, his life, they were discussing. Tears burned the back of her eyelids, and she looked up at him, her heart in her throat. His gaze caught hers, questioning, lingering, then he visibly flinched and jerked his head back toward the other ranger.

"You talked to Goldenrod?" Ranger McQuade asked.

Hayes shook his head. "No, he's out of town. Margaret said he'll be back Saturday for the big party." He gave Taylor a scathing look. "Which I think you should cancel."

Taylor opened her mouth to reply, but Ranger McQuade spoke first. "No, let her have it. All the major players will be present. Something may happen."

"That's what I'm worried about," Hayes said. "There will be too many people in one room. It'll be harder to protect Taylor."

"We'll all be there for extra security," Brody said.

Hayes nodded, his expression stony. He obviously wanted to end the investigation so he could leave Cantara Hills. Leave Margaret and her behind.

Taylor sipped her wine. She didn't know why that thought bothered her so badly.

Because she wanted him to forgive Margaret, to have a relationship with her best friend?

Or because she wanted time to make him fall in love with her?

THE NEXT DAY, TENSION tightened Hayes's shoulders as he entered the ballroom inside Taylor's estate with Taylor on her arm. She looked stunning in the emerald-green satin ball gown that showcased her curves and cleavage.

Hellacious desires bombarded him. The woman was torturing him. The night before she'd been almost solicitous. Sweet, smiling at him, offering him a cold beer—a beer, for God's sake, when he figured the woman wouldn't allow it in her house. And that dinner she'd prepared had been mouthwatering.

Gorgeous and she could cook…

Was she as good in bed as she was in the kitchen?

Today, watching her calmly organize the details of the event tonight, he'd realized that she was…amazing. Organized and businesslike, but kind and respectful to the vendors and staff, treating them almost like friends or respected coworkers, not as if they were her underlings. And she cared about Margaret.

Still, she was way out of his league.

He tugged at the tie to the suit she'd had sent over for him, feeling completely out of place. He wanted his jeans and Stetson.

But Taylor had argued that if he wore the suit, he'd blend in.

He didn't want to blend in.

Except that out of uniform he'd put the guests more at ease, and maybe catch them off guard.

Taylor smiled at him from across the room, and his heart tripped. Hell, he was a red-blooded man and he wanted Taylor Landis. At least his body did. His mind protested, but his hunger seemed destined to ignore logic.

For the next hour, he followed her around like a damn puppy, making sure she was safe, yet salivating as she greeted strangers with a hug. These people were her friends, her kind of people.

He wasn't.

And of course, every man in the room appeared smitten with her, which only stoked his irritation as the night wore on.

Violin and piano music played from the orchestra on the stage and an ice statue of two doves created a centerpiece. Flowing chocolate fountains were interspersed throughout the room, along with dozens of fresh flower arrangements.

Food he'd never heard of or considered eating was artfully arranged on white linen tablecloths, and waiters dressed in monkey suits carried silver trays laden with appetizers, crystal flutes of champagne, wine and martinis. The attendees wore glitzy evening gowns and tuxes, and diamonds and other gemstones glittered beneath the chandeliers.

His stomach growled for a burger and brewsky.

But he wasn't here as a guest, he reminded himself, just to guard Taylor and investigate her friends. Link Hathaway, dressed in a gray tux that matched his silver-gray hair, stood by a staging area, watching his daughter as if he was afraid Hayes might get too close to her. Margaret smiled at him across the room, although sadness flickered in her eyes when he didn't return the gesture, and his gut clenched. Pretty boy Goldenrod had arrived with her, his manicured hand lying possessively across her back as they wove through the crowd.

Against the women's wishes, Brody and Egan had kept Victoria and Caroline away, but they insisted they would attend the wedding. Hopefully, the Rangers would have solved this case and Hayes and the Rangers could skip the ceremony. He didn't want to be anywhere near that shindig—instead he'd be riding his horse across his land while his birth mother married into politics.

Kenneth and Tammy Sutton rolled in to applause, although Hayes noticed Goldenrod's smile seemed forced.

Was there tension between the two men? And if so, why?

Politics? Maybe something to do with those illegal bids? Or was it personal?

A cloud of perfume swirled around Tammy Sutton as she glided past him, but she ignored him as if he was invisible and swept Taylor into a hug. "This is marvelous, darling. You always throw the best parties, Taylor. I don't know what we'd do without you around here."

"Thanks, Tammy," Taylor said. "I'm so glad you and Kenneth could make it. I understand how busy your schedule has been with the campaign."

"Yes," Tammy said, brushing a bejeweled hand up to pat her husband's cheek. "It has been hectic, but well worth it. Soon Kenneth will be sitting in the governor's chair where he belongs."

Or in jail, Hayes thought sourly.

"I know," Taylor agreed. "It's an exciting time for both of you."

Kenneth took Taylor's hands in his. "I couldn't have accomplished all I did for the city council without a great team. I'll be forever grateful to you, Taylor."

Taylor smiled. "Of course. You know you've earned my loyalty."

Link Hathaway moved up beside Devon Goldenrod while Margaret approached Taylor. "This is lovely, Taylor." She glanced at him, a softness in her eyes that twisted at him. "I'm glad you're here, Hayes."

"I'm here to protect Taylor, nothing more," Hayes said curtly.

Taylor glared at him, and Margaret's smile faltered. "I know, and I'm thankful for that. She doesn't deserve to be in danger, especially because she was trying to do something nice for me."

He couldn't argue with her over that, or stand to see her looking at him as if she wanted his forgiveness, so he excused himself. He needed to focus, to talk to Goldenrod.

Eyes trained on the man, he cut him off before Hathaway reached him, although he had no doubt that Margaret's father had already warned Goldenrod that Hayes would be asking questions.

He wanted to observe the man's reaction personally. Feel him out and see if he had a hidden agenda.

Did he love Margaret?

Hayes adjusted his tie, a smile cracking his lips when he noticed Goldenrod's thumb raking up and down the stem of his champagne flute as if he was nervous.

"Mr. Goldenrod," Hayes said. "I'm Ranger Keller."

"I know who you are," Goldenrod said with an edge to his voice that indicated he was also aware that he was Margaret's son.

"Then you realize why I'm here."

"Because you want access to Margaret's wealth."

Anger surged through Hayes. "No, because of the attempt on Taylor Landis's life and Morris's murder. I intend to find the person responsible and lock him behind bars."

The two of them indulged in a stare-off for several tense seconds.

"I don't know how I can help you."

"Do you own a gun?" Hayes asked.

Goldenrod shook his head. "No. Haven't felt the need."

"Where were you night before last?"

"Why are you asking?"

"Don't play dumb," Hayes said. "Even if Margaret didn't tell you about my visit to her and her father, Hathaway did. You know the private investigator who was working for Taylor was murdered."

"I was in Houston," Goldenrod said. "On business."

"I suppose you have witnesses?"

He nodded, not a blade of his sandy-blond hair moving. "A roomful."

Hayes twisted his mouth in thought. For some reason he didn't like this man. Didn't trust him.

"Now, I suggest you leave me and Margaret alone," Goldenrod said, dropping his voice a decibel. "She and I are to be wed, and I don't intend to let anything stop the ceremony." His eyes glinted like ice. "I won't allow you to cause trouble for her or hurt her."

Hayes raised a brow. That was rich, Goldenrod threatening him.

"Do you understand what I'm saying?" Goldenrod asked.

Hayes gritted his teeth at the bastard. "Oh, yeah, I hear you." He pushed his face into Goldenrod's. "But you don't scare me, pretty boy. And if you had anything to do with the attacks on Taylor, then I'll lock your ass up and throw away the key."

He stormed away, leaving Goldenrod with that message. When he looked up, Margaret was watching, her face lined with concern.

The tinkle of spoons clinking against glass rippled through the air, and voices began to hush. Taylor walked up the steps to the stage, her delicious curves mesmerizing him as she took the microphone. "I want to welcome you all to the party tonight. We're here to honor my best friend Margaret Hathaway and her fiancé, Devon Goldenrod. Let's raise our glasses to toast their upcoming nuptials."

Taylor lifted her glass and a chorus of shouts rang out as guests whispered and cheered. Link Hathaway climbed the steps, a smile stretching across his face.

But suddenly a shot rang out, shattering the ice statue on stage, and chaos erupted. Guests screamed and ducked, running from the room.

Hayes jerked his gun from his holster, and yelled for Taylor to get down as another bullet zoomed toward her.

Chapter Seventeen

Taylor screamed and ducked behind the statue, and Link Hathaway dashed down the steps toward Margaret. Guests yelled and ran, glasses shattered on the floor as people scurried for safety and another shot flew by her head.

"Stay down, Taylor!" Hayes braced his gun to fire as he scanned the room, then he must have zeroed in on the shooter's location because he ran toward the side entry to the stage behind a curtained off area, vaulted through the opening and fired a shot.

She couldn't see what was happening, only hear the panicked sounds of the guests and Margaret calling her name. But when she looked up, Link and Devon Goldenrod had sequestered Margaret between them. And the other Rangers were searching the room.

It seemed like hours but only seconds passed when another shot rang out, and Taylor cried out again, terrified Hayes had been hit.

Her chest ached from the pressure of holding her breath, then he finally appeared, shoving her brother in front of him.

Taylor gasped. Miles was handcuffed and spitting out curse words. "Miles?"

"I'm sorry, Taylor," Hayes said in a gruff voice. "But he was the shooter."

"This is your fault, you bitch!" Miles lifted his hand, his shaggy brown hair falling over one eye.

"Why?" Taylor gasped. "Why would you try to kill me?"

He jerked his head around, gesturing at the room. "You spend all this money for a party and you won't help me. It's not fair."

Taylor's chest clenched, but anger assaulted her. "You had your own money, Miles, and you threw it away, wasted it on drugs and gambling when you could have done something with your life. Could have helped others."

Margaret hurried to her side for support, and Hayes sent her a look of regret, but she didn't blame him. Her own brother had tried to kill her, and he could have hurt others. She refused to allow Miles to make her feel guilty for his problems.

"Come on, Landis," Hayes growled. "You have an appointment with a cell tonight."

He shoved Miles through the crowd of guests who were finally settling down with hushed whispers after the chaos.

"Taylor, maybe everyone should leave," Margaret said.

Taylor shook her head. "I don't want this to spoil your night."

Margaret gripped her hands. "Honey, you are so much more important than a party. And I know you're upset about Miles."

Taylor glanced around, saw that the guests were uncomfortable. Plus the room was a mess—broken glass splattered on the floor, flutes overturned and food trays wrecked.

Tears stung her eyes and embarrassment flooded her cheeks, but she blinked back the tears, held her head up high and walked back to the microphone. "Please forgive me for what just happened," she said, her voice steadier than her legs. "I apologize for my brother's actions and sincerely hope that everyone is all right. Under the circumstances, though, I suggest we call it a night."

Hayes pushed Miles from the room, and locked gazes with Taylor.

Once he took Miles into custody, he could close the investigation and life could return to normal.

Relief tickled her, yet a deep ache throbbed in her chest. Then Hayes would leave Cantara Hills and she would never see him again.

HAYES HATED THE PAIN in Taylor's eyes and wanted to throttle her brother for hurting her. The stupid arrogant little twit. He had money and family and he'd screwed all of it.

Brody and Egan hurried to calm the guests and make sure they departed safely.

"Stop shoving me," Miles growled.

"You should be grateful I didn't blow your damn head off, you idiot."

Miles glared at him with hate-filled eyes, and Hayes tightened his grip on the man's hands.

Voices echoed from the foyer, guests leaving, Taylor

saying goodbye and thanking people for attending, car engines revving up and rolling away.

Brody met him at the exit. Hayes opened the side door and led Miles toward him. Miles actually jerked his arm, seeming to have the stupid idea that he might run.

Hayes dug his fingers deeper into the guy's arm. "I'll take him in," Brody said. "You should stay."

Hayes removed Miles's gun from where he'd tucked it in the waistband of his jeans. "I'm sure you'll find GSR on his hands, too."

"It's a .38," Brody said. "I'll see if it matches the other bullet casings we found."

"I'll go search for the bullet casings and send them over."

Brody nodded, then took custody of Miles, who gave Hayes another bitter look before Brody shut the car door.

"I'll keep you posted," Brody said.

Hayes nodded. He wanted to question the jerk himself, but Taylor was upset, and his gut warned him that she didn't need to be left alone. Not tonight.

Besides, what if Miles had only reacted this evening, and wasn't the man they were looking for? They had to tie up loose ends and make certain the threat to Taylor was over.

Then he could leave.

He strode back to the ballroom and spent the next half hour searching for the bullet casings. He dug one out of the stage floor, another from the wall only inches from where Taylor had stood, then another from behind the staging area. If Miles had hit her, Taylor might be dead.

A frisson of fear ripped through him and sweat beaded on his forehead. He didn't want to see her hurt. Not physically, by a bullet.

And not by her brother because families should stick together.

Not that he knew anything about families….

The waitstaff for the party had begun cleaning up and taking down the bar. He bagged the bullets to send to forensics, then headed back toward the entrance when Margaret appeared.

"Hayes?"

He froze, heart pounding. "Yes?"

"Thank you for saving Taylor tonight." Emotions glittered in her eyes. "I was terrified for her."

He gave a clipped nod. "I'm glad she's all right, ma'am."

Ma'am? This was his mother. Yet he barely knew her. Would never be able to call her that.

"I'm not sure she is," Margaret said gently. "Taylor appears tough and strong, but having her own brother shoot at her…that cut deep."

He supposed it would. "He's in custody now. He can't hurt her again."

"Well…" She hesitated as if she wanted to say more, then Goldenrod appeared behind her, and placed a protective hand at her waist.

Hayes gritted his teeth. Goldenrod had made it clear he didn't want Hayes near Margaret.

"Please take care of her tonight," Margaret said. "She seems all right now but it'll hit her later."

"Don't worry," Hayes said. "I'll stay with her."

Margaret's eyes softened with relief, and she turned

to leave with Goldenrod. He watched her go, feeling an odd sensation in his chest.

And that strange sense of panic that maybe Taylor was still in danger.

TAYLOR HUGGED MARGARET good-night, then forced herself to face the staff she'd hired for the party and oversee the cleanup. Emotions ping-ponged inside her as she remembered the frenetic scene that had erupted when that shot had rung out.

She still couldn't believe that Miles had tried to shoot her. He would face charges now, perhaps spend time in jail....

Her father would be crushed. Angry. And even more remote than he had been the past few years.

She only hoped that he would make sure Miles received the therapy he needed to get his act together.

And poor Margaret...she already felt the strain of finding out that Hayes was her son, and Taylor had sensed tension between her and Devon and Hayes all evening.

Tonight's episode certainly hadn't helped.

"I think we have things covered," the caterer said. "We'll bill you as usual."

Taylor thanked the woman, then sighed and left the ballroom. Hayes was talking to Ranger Caldwell, and handed him the bullet casings to take to the lab.

"I'll check in with you tomorrow," Hayes said.

Ranger Caldwell nodded and left, and Taylor bypassed him and headed up the staircase. She wanted a shower, to wash the scent of fear off her body, to warm herself so she could finally stop trembling.

She ripped the hairpins from the bun at the base of her neck, tossed them on her dresser, then removed her diamonds and placed them in her jewelry box.

Then she stripped her gown and walked into the bathroom, flipped on the shower and climbed inside. The tears fell as she drowned herself in the warm spray, her body shaking from the aftermath of the night.

She allowed herself to spend her emotions and scrubbed with her favorite bodywash, willing away the image of her brother in handcuffs, but memories of the night she'd almost been strangled haunted her. Had Miles done that, too?

She donned a robe and walked into her bedroom, wondering how she would sleep in her house tonight.

When she entered the bedroom, Hayes was standing by her bed, looking concerned. "I knocked, but you didn't answer so I got worried." His voice was low, husky. "Are you all right, Taylor?"

She clutched the thin robe to her, her body tingling as his gaze raked over her. She was still cold, still trembling, still felt so damn vulnerable. "Yes."

His eyes narrowed. "You're lying."

"I will be fine," she whispered. "I just need some time."

Hayes lifted his hand and tucked a strand of hair behind her ear. The movement was so gentle that she shivered, but not from being cold, from arousal.

"I understand that Miles is family." He rubbed his thumb down her cheek. "I'm sorry I had to arrest him."

"It's not your fault," Taylor said. "He was out of control. He could have hurt someone...me, Margaret...you..."

"Shh, he didn't, though," Hayes said. "Margaret is safe and so are you."

They stared at one another, emotions pummeling her as she felt his arms encircle her.

She slid her arms beneath his, clutched his back and breathed in his scent. He smelled like a man, masculine, rugged, strong. And he held her with such tenderness that her heart swelled. Beneath that tough facade and badge, his heart beat strong and solid. He was a good man. The kind heroes were made of.

Heaven help her, she was falling in love with this cowboy.

But he would leave soon. Ride out of town and never come back. She couldn't let him go without tasting him again. Without a night in his arms where she could show him that they could fit together.

She licked her lips, cradled his face between her hands and dragged his head toward her. He stiffened, but she fused her mouth with his and traced her tongue over his lips. He moaned deep in his throat, then his hands slid lower to yank her against him. She felt his hard length press into her, and knew he wanted her.

ADRENALINE WAS STILL CHURNING through Hayes, that and the fear that had robbed his breath when the shot had broken out. He hadn't been able to reach Taylor fast enough.

And now…now all he'd meant to do was comfort her. But those damn lips teased him, and so had the sight of her in that skimpy robe. Her nipples were tight, turgid peaks, the sheer fabric giving him a glimpse of her pale-pink areolas beneath. He wanted his mouth on them.

And his hands on the rest of her naked flesh.

She licked at his jaw and rubbed her foot up his calf, and his arousal stabbed the fly of his damn suit pants.

He had to stop this insanity.

He forced himself to pull away but she gripped his arms and kept him from leaving.

Still, his chest was pounding. "Taylor, you're scared. Tonight was traumatic." His voice cracked. He was a ranger first, had to take charge, stay in control. "I can't take advantage of you."

"You're not," she murmured raggedly. "I want you, Hayes. Please make love to me."

"Taylor…"

Her breath brushed his cheek as she kissed him again, robbing him of words, of anything but the raw primal lust burning inside him.

Then she teased his lips with her tongue again. He opened, so starved for her that he murmured her name and trailed his hands over her breasts, deepening the kiss as he stroked her nipples through the satiny robe. The buds hardened to peaks, her chest rising and falling erratically, arousing sensations that rippled through every muscle in his body.

"I want your hands and mouth on me," she said into his throat. "And you inside me."

No woman had ever talked to him like that. Had ever sounded so starved for him. So passionate….

He parted the fabric, rubbed his thumbs over the turgid peaks, then lowered his head and licked the tip. She gasped and thrust herself at him, clinging to him as if she'd fall apart if he released her.

He sucked one nipple into his mouth, stroked his hand over her hips, then to her inner thigh where he feathered his fingers along the delicate skin of her legs, parting them slightly to allow him better access to her precious secrets. Heat shot through him, firing his sex to a raging need that destroyed any common sense.

"Yes," she rasped. "Take me, Hayes. I need you."

His breath caught and he dragged his mouth from her breast to watch as she dropped the flimsy robe to the floor and stood beautifully naked before him.

Chapter Eighteen

Hayes paused to drink in Taylor's beauty, his chest heaving with the need to make love to her. She reached for his tie and yanked it off, then tossed it to the floor. Her hands tore at his dress shirt, buttons flying as she hastily pushed it off his shoulders and slung it behind her. As soon as her fingers began to fumble with his belt and zipper, he thought he would explode.

But he reined in the need raging through him, kicked off his shoes, then shoved off his pants and socks.

"Hayes…"

Taylor's whispered sigh spiked his hunger, and when she kissed him again, he backed her against the wall, taking all that she offered as her tongue danced with his.

She tasted so delicious that he groaned, and raked his hands over her shoulders, her back, her breasts again, his sex throbbing with the need to stroke her, to fill her, to make her his.

He tore his mouth away, and her breath bathed his neck as he lowered his head and teased her nipples again with his tongue, sipping greedily as her hair brushed his neck. Her scent made his heart race, and he trailed kisses down her abdomen to her thighs and teased the sensitive skin guarding her secrets.

She moaned and clawed her hands through his hair, and he used his tongue as he would his length to slide between her legs and tease her until she parted her legs. Then he plunged his tongue inside her to taste her sweet essence.

"Hayes…"

He held her still, his movements bolder, his own excitement growing hotter as she whispered her pleasure and offered herself to him. Seconds later, her body quivered beneath his onslaught, and her wet juices filled his mouth, a taste so erotic he would never forget the headiness.

Or how much he wanted her.

DIZZY WITH THE BLINDING sensations spiraling through her, Taylor closed her eyes and relented to the intense climax riding through her, a climax made more satisfying and erotic by her growing feelings for Hayes.

Tears threatened, but she blinked them away, quivering as Hayes's mouth played havoc with her senses. He held her, loved her, pleasured her as if she was a fine treasure he'd found, one that was meant to be treated with loving care. A fire erupted deep inside her belly, flaming hotter with each sensation exploding through her and burning out of control.

She clawed at his arms, dragged him back up to stand, then lowered her hand and stroked his hard length. He was huge, bulging beneath the boxers, and she was frantic to feel his naked flesh inside her, frantic to pleasure him as he had her.

She breathed, her passion spiraling out of control,

and pulled at the boxers, freeing him so she felt the damp fullness of his erection pulsing with need. She moved to go down on him, but he caught her arms, kicked off his boxers and lifted her. She looped her arms around him and rubbed her wet, aching heat against his hard length, begging him to take her.

"Taylor… I want you now."

"Yes," she pleaded. "I need you, Hayes."

He moaned, deep and throaty, hunger lacing the sound, then tore away from her.

"Can't," he muttered gruffly. "No condom."

"The nightstand," she whispered, and he grinned and reached inside the drawer and ripped one out, her legs still wrapped around him.

They laughed together as she tried to help him roll it on, his huge size making it difficult. The flare of raw passion in his eyes heated her skin and ignited her desires to a frenzied fever.

She threw her head back in wild abandon, then tightened her legs around his waist, crying out his name as she impaled herself on him.

He growled, pushing deeper, gripping her legs as he thrust farther into her warm chamber. She lifted her hips, angling herself to feel him pulse against her sensitive nub, her breath erratic as he pulled himself out, then thrust again, more forcefully this time, delving deeper into her body until she panted his name again. Perspiration dotted her skin as she rode him up and down.

Any semblance of control evaporated like rain on hot pavement. The sounds of their bodies slapping together, their husky whispers and choppy breathing filled the room. Raw, primal, sensual noises that intensified the trembling in her body and sent another mind-shattering climax to overtake her.

Her insides clenched, and he thrust into her again, their bodies climbing to the heavens together as his own orgasm ripped through him.

The erotic outpouring rippled in wave after wave of mind-numbing pleasure until Taylor dropped her head forward against his neck, heaving for a breath. He leaned into her, his face buried between her breasts, as his body shook from the pleasure.

They stood like that for what seemed like hours, each drawing in breaths, holding each other, their bodies entwined, her heart soaring with love. Finally he carried her to bed and they fell onto it, exhausted. But she curled into his arms and he wrapped them around her and held her.

Emotions overwhelmed her, feelings that ripped away the fear she'd had earlier, yet another fear fought its way through the clouded recesses of her pleasure.

Hayes would leave soon, and she couldn't stand to lose him.

No man had ever made her feel this heartfelt knot of love and happiness bursting inside her.

She had to find a way to convince him that they belonged together.

SUNLIGHT STREAKED THE SKY as Hayes stirred from a deep sleep. He smiled, sensations rocketing through him. He was dreaming. Dreaming of having sex with Taylor. Featherlight strokes massaged his hard length, a damp tongue laving him. He opened his eyes and groaned as erotic tension pummeled him. He wasn't dreaming.

Taylor had crawled beneath the covers and was going down on him. Had his throbbing length inside her mouth, wetting it with her tongue, sucking it, applying pressure...

He threw the covers back with a guttural groan, the sight of her long blond hair spilled across his bare belly sending a shot of pure lust through him. She trailed her tongue along his length, teasing the tip, her other hand massaging the insides of his thighs, stoking him to degrees of pain-pleasure that made her name rip from deep in his throat.

If she continued, he was going to lose it.

"Taylor, honey, you have to stop...."

She lifted her head, her eyes hooded and dark with desire, and his excitement skyrocketed. "No," she said softly.

He shook his head as she closed her mouth around him again. Her warm wet mouth enflamed him, and he clenched the sheets, struggling for control. But she was determined to torture him. She sucked him long and hard, riding up and down until he forced her to stop.

"I want inside you," he said gruffly.

She laughed, reached for a condom and ripped it open. They barely got it on before she crawled on top of him and straddled him. With one hand she guided his throbbing member inside her. Her beautiful breasts fell heavy in front of him and he leaned on his elbows, biting at her nipples, licking and drawing one into his mouth as she moved up and down on him. She tossed her hair over her shoulder, crying his name as spasms made her insides clench tighter around him.

Unable to stand the tension any longer, he threw his

head back, gripped her hips and they found a frenzied passionate rhythm that sent them both over the edge together.

Her breathing erratic, she collapsed on top of him, their sweat mingling, their bodies still joined, and he closed his arms around her. Holy hell, he could get used to waking up like this.

No, he couldn't fantasize about other mornings with Taylor on top of him.

"That was so wonderful." Taylor pressed a kiss to his chest, stroking him.

"I thought I was dreaming when I woke up," he mumbled gruffly.

She laughed against his chest. "See how good we are together, Hayes?"

Something about her tone flamed his desire again, but fear also darted through him. He couldn't let her think this was anything but sex. That he would stick around after the investigation.

He'd go back to his world and she would return to hers. He wouldn't allow himself to think otherwise or to offer her hope of more.

Margaret's wedding was Saturday. With Miles in jail, and loose ends still unclear, he'd take her away to his place until the wedding. Maybe by then they'd know for sure if the danger to her was over.

When she saw how he lived, his lifestyle, she'd realize that the two of them weren't suited at all.

Except in bed...and there he'd found a slice of heaven.

WHILE HAYES SHOWERED, Taylor slid from bed and prepared breakfast, then placed it on a bed tray and carried it back to her bedroom. When Hayes emerged from the shower, his hair damp, a towel knotted around his waist, her mouth watered.

"That looks delicious," he said.

"So do you."

His gaze locked with hers, heat and memories of their lovemaking lighting the flames of desire again. But his stomach growled, and she put her needs on hold and patted the bed.

"Sit and eat, Hayes. You're going to need your energy again later."

A chuckle rumbled from his chest. "Is that so?"

She nodded, plucked a fresh strawberry from the tray and offered it to him. He sucked it into his mouth, licking the tip of her fingers when he was finished, then he joined her on the bed and they devoured the omelet and muffins.

She raked her hands over his chest. "Now, I want you again."

He gripped her hands. "Taylor, Egan and Brody are going to interrogate Miles today and hope to tie up loose ends. Why don't we ride out to my place, get out of Cantara Hills till the dust settles?"

"We'll be back for Margaret's rehearsal dinner?"

"Yeah. But the press will probably be all over Miles's arrest and will hound you. I thought it might do you good to get away."

Her heart stuttered. "Oh, goodness. I'm not ready for the media circus. Not yet…."

He nodded. "Then pack a bag."

She grabbed his hand and kissed it. "Thank you, Hayes. I'm looking forward to seeing your home."

Affection flickered in his eyes, and he twisted his mouth, uncomfortable. "I'll call Brody and tell him where we'll be while you get dressed. Oh, and pack casual, jeans if you have them. My place is country, not country club."

She winced at his comment, but blew it off. Did he think she didn't like the country? That she had to have a mansion?

She kissed him, then hurried to the shower, determined to prove him wrong. Hayes must be starting to have feelings for her, otherwise he wouldn't invite her to his home.

She couldn't think of anything nicer than leaving town with him, getting away from the ugliness of the investigation. A place where no one could bother them, and she and Hayes could make love day and night.

Where she could prove to him they had a future.

HAYES BRACED HIMSELF for Taylor's reaction as they drove to his cabin. Rustic would best describe the home he'd built for himself. He liked the open space, pasture for his horses, the huge ancient trees with their gnarled branches, the stream where he could fish and the peace and quiet of the land.

There was no sauna, outdoor swimming pool, marble in the bathroom nor gourmet kitchen. A woodstove served as the main heat source in the winter although he had installed central air for the unbearably hot summers.

He'd added the front porch at the last minute so he could enjoy coffee and morning sunrises.

As soon as he pulled down the three-mile drive to his

secluded property, Taylor perked up, a smile spreading across her face that shocked him and caught him off guard.

"Oh my God, this is breathtaking, Hayes. I can't believe you own it."

He swallowed, gripping the steering wheel tighter. "It's not fancy, Taylor."

He maneuvered the gravel road, still expecting her to look down on his cabin, but she "oohed" and "aahed" as he parked, her exuberance making his heart pick up a notch.

"This is wonderful, Hayes. So secluded and quiet and, oh, look at that stream in back and your horses." She clapped her hands, unfastened her seat belt, jumped out and jogged over to the gate.

Apache trotted straight to her like a pathetic love-struck male, whinnied and nuzzled up to her as she petted him.

Hayes grimaced. He was in deep trouble, had vastly underestimated Taylor Landis.

Tucking his hands in the pockets of his jeans, he loped over to the fence, glaring at Apache.

"He's gorgeous," Taylor said, her face glowing with excitement. "Can we ride while we're here?"

"You ride?" he croaked, then figured she rode dressage, show horses if anything, not trail riding.

"I love to ride," she said with such a softness to her voice that her sincerity rang through loud and clear. "Each year, I host a summer camp for handicapped and underprivileged children at a ranch." She turned to him, eyes sparkling with emotion. "Maybe this next year, you can come and visit with the children."

His gut clenched, emotions that he didn't want hitting him. He'd thought Taylor a rich snotty heiress, yet she offered more than money to her charities. She gave her time and her heart.

A heart that he was beginning to fall for.

He sucked in a sharp breath. Remembered how he'd awakened this morning with her loving him. Remembered the delicious way she tasted and how sweetly she'd offered herself to him.

Remembered that someone wanted to kill her.

That would not happen. If it did, it would be over his dead body.

Chapter Nineteen

Taylor spent the next few days in total bliss. Two days of relaxation, picnics outside, wading in the stream, riding across his property on horseback, feeding each other in bed and making love.

He was surprised when she'd saddled her own horse, and even more so at the way she settled into his home. It was cozy and comfortable, with wood floors, braided rugs, a fireplace and handmade quilts on his massive oak bed. He'd built most of the furniture himself including the rocking chair by the fireplace and the porch swing where they sipped their coffee.

All the place needed was a cat curled in the corner and a couple of children running in the yard. *A little boy with dark hair and big dark eyes....*

Their last night together, their lovemaking felt even more frantic as they both felt the clock counting down the minutes until they had to return to Cantara Hills, to reality and the investigation.

He took her against the wall, on the floor, outside on his back porch with the stars twinkling above the Texas sky, his horses prancing across the open pasture and coyotes howling in the distance.

During the ride back to her estate, Taylor broached the subject of Margaret again. "Please give her a chance," she said. "She cares about you, Hayes."

"But she still hasn't told me my father's name," he said bitterly.

"She will, Hayes, just give her time."

He grunted, and Taylor bit her lip, the rest of the ride strained and silent.

Finally, as they pulled into her drive, Hayes cleared his throat. "I talked to Brody this morning while you showered. Your father showed up with a lawyer. Miles admits to the shooting at the party, but not to Morris's murder or the pool attack. We did find your charm bracelet at his house, though."

She sighed. "He knew that would hurt me."

He nodded. "But this means that you could still be in danger, Taylor."

Fear slithered through her. "Then you won't leave yet?"

He studied her, his expression indicating that he heard the double meaning underlying her words.

"No, not yet."

She nodded, a sharp pain clawing at her heart. She'd intended to tell him that she loved him at the ranch, but had decided to hold back, to show him instead of saying the words. And she thought she had.

She only hoped it was enough.

"What time is the rehearsal dinner?" Hayes asked.

"Seven." She climbed from the car. She had a million things to do before then.

The rest of the day flew by. She had lunch with

Margaret and an appointment to pick up her dress. Hayes tagged along, looking awkward and quiet but so damn handsome that she could barely keep her eyes off of him.

Margaret traced a finger along her water glass. "Last night I told Devon that I'm meeting with Hayes's father to tell him about Hayes."

"How did Devon react?" Taylor asked.

"Not well. He begged me to reconsider." Anguish laced Margaret's voice. "But I think he should know, and Hayes has a right to know his birth father's identity."

"Devon probably just feels threatened," Taylor said softly.

Margaret's face looked pinched. "I know. But it's not like Hayes's father wants me. He's married."

Taylor sighed. "I'm sorry. Are you going to see his father before the wedding?"

Worry filled Margaret's eyes as she glanced at Hayes where he stood by the wall of the restaurant. "Right after I leave here. I'm not looking forward to it."

"Good luck, Margaret." Taylor squeezed her hand. "And call me if you need me."

"I will."

Taylor murmured a silent prayer for her friend as Margaret left. She still hoped Hayes would come around. Maybe if she and he stayed together...

If they married...

With visions of the two of them celebrating their own ceremony on his ranch in her head, she rushed to her spa appointment. Her father phoned during her massage and she called him back on the way to the hair salon. "Are you all right, Taylor?"

She bit her lip at his concerned tone. "Yes, Dad."

"I can't believe Miles tried to hurt you."

Tears blurred her eyes. "It was awful. He needs help."

"And he'll get it. But he may have to spend some time in jail to learn his lesson."

At least he wasn't going to let Miles off this time.

"Do you want me to come to the house tonight, Taylor?"

"No. Ranger Keller is there."

"He'd better take care of you," her father said.

She smiled, although she wondered how her father would react if he knew about them.

After she hung up, she met with the hairstylist. Hayes waited in the lobby, his dark look imposing, reminding her that someone still wanted her dead.

He also looked bored and disgusted, triggering anxiety to sprout again in her belly. Was she being foolish to hope that he loved her?

As she dressed for the rehearsal dinner that evening, anxiety riddled her. Hayes met her at the bottom of the steps wearing his Stetson and jeans as if to remind her again that they belonged to different worlds, that he wasn't here as a guest but as her bodyguard. She had fit into his world fine.

Would he even try to fit into hers?

She struggled to stifle her doubts as he drove her to the church for the rehearsal. The stained-glass cathedral with its ornate windows and candelabras looked stunning with candles burning, but Margaret acted nervous and fidgety, and she and Devon both looked strained as they went through the motions of the rehearsal.

Twice she caught Hayes watching Margaret with

an odd look in his eyes, and she wondered if he might be softening.

She stumbled, the strap of her heel slipping free. He caught her, and she gazed into his eyes, heat rippling between them as she recalled their erotic lovemaking. His hands stroking and touching her, his mouth loving her body from her head to her toes, the two of them riding each other day and night.

"Are you all right?" he asked gruffly.

She licked her lips. "Yes. Just hot."

A smile twitched at his mouth. "It is hot in here," he agreed in a low voice.

She smiled and he knelt and fastened her shoe for her, his finger tracing a path along her bare toes that sent a chill of longing through her. "Later," she whispered.

He stared at her, but he didn't answer.

When they arrived at the country club, a host of cars filed down the drive, and two reporters with cameras stood on the entrance steps. Margaret Hathaway's marriage was society news, especially with Devon running for city council and Kenneth in attendance. Camera lights flashed as Devon and Margaret exited their limo, and they paused to pose for photos and to address the reporters.

Taylor hung back in the car, allowing them their moment, and curious about how Margaret's talk with Hayes's father went.

Finally satisfied they'd given the press what they'd come for, one of the reporters moved to interview other guests.

Hayes accepted the parking stub from the valet and she climbed out. He circled around the car to accompany her, but just as they reached the top of the steps and neared the entrance, the other reporter zoomed toward her. Cameras flashed, capturing her on Hayes's arm and she smiled, but felt Hayes stiffen.

"Miss Landis, Connie Winstead. We heard your brother was arrested for attempted murder."

Hayes cleared his throat, but Taylor spoke up, aware she had to deal with the fallout. "Yes, that's true. Unfortunately, my brother has some emotional difficulties. The family is going to do all we can to support his recovery."

"Is it true that Texas Rangers have been assigned to protect you?" The reporter pivoted toward Hayes with a raised brow.

Taylor swallowed but kept her smile intact. "Yes, temporarily."

Connie leaned closer with a wink. "We also heard that the two of you went away together. Give us the scoop, Miss Landis. We heard two of Cantara Hills' finest residents have become engaged to rangers. Is there a romantic relationship between you and Ranger Keller?"

Taylor barely restrained a gasp. Hayes stiffened, looking intimidating and furious, while she glanced up and saw Margaret watching her with interest. She couldn't very well divulge such personal information in front of the press.

"Ranger Keller simply escorted me to a safe place to allow me to get away for a few days."

A devious look sparkled in Connie's eyes. "So you're not having an affair with Ranger Keller?"

"Certainly not," Taylor said matter-of-factly. "Now, please excuse me. This is Miss Hathaway's rehearsal dinner."

At that moment, Kenneth and Tammy Sutton rolled up, someone shrieked about their arrival and the reporters darted toward them.

She swept forward, and Hayes followed, his expression stoic. Taylor pulled Hayes into the entryway and headed to the ladies' room to recover.

HAYES FISTED HIS HANDS by his sides to control his raging temper. He'd never been rough with a woman before but he'd wanted to grab that damn woman reporter and shake her senseless. And Taylor…he'd been poleaxed by the reporter's questions, but she had remained cool, aloof, had replied without even thinking about her answer.

Because she'd never admit to her friends and social circle that she'd stooped low enough to bed a cowboy.

All that lovemaking this weekend, those sweet smiles, intimate moments, how she'd pretended to like his cabin and ranch…she'd just been slumming.

"Hayes, I'm sorry about that," she said. "I wasn't expecting the press to be interested in me tonight."

"Why not?" he growled. "You're high-society news, Taylor. You always will be in the spotlight."

She frowned at his cutting tone. "That may be true, but I don't like my personal life plastered across the papers for everyone in the world to read."

"No, I don't imagine you'd want people knowing you slummed with me."

Her eyes widened, anger sparking. "Slummed?"

He shrugged. "That's what you did, didn't you? Wanted to see how the other half lived?"

"That's ridiculous." She grabbed his arm. "I enjoyed

every minute we spent together, Hayes. And making love to you had nothing to do with wanting to see how the other half lived. I'm in love with you."

"Right." He made a throaty sound of disbelief. "Don't confuse love with sex, Taylor. That's all we had together. Great sex."

"It was great," she said, her voice breaking. "Great because I love you, Hayes. Because we're good together."

"It was great sex," he said through clenched teeth, "because someone taught you how to pleasure a man, Taylor."

Hurt flickered across her face, and tears pooled in her eyes. He felt like a jerk, but he couldn't retract the words. It had been painfully obvious that she didn't want her friends to know she'd been intimate with him. He hadn't expected different, but these past few days, for a few moments, he'd almost allowed himself to forget who she was. Where she'd come from. Where he'd come from.

That they had no future together.

She spun around, swiping at the tears, then bolted inside the ladies' room.

His stomach churned, but he watched her go. They had to part when the case ended, anyway. No use living a fantasy that wouldn't come true.

She'd realize he was right in no time, and then she'd move on to a man of her caliber.

And he'd be alone again, just as he always had been. Just as he liked it.

TAYLOR FELT LIKE THE BIGGEST fool in the world. Hayes didn't love her, didn't see her as anything more than a good lay that he'd enjoyed on the job.

She wiped at the tears, sucked in a deep breath and reminded herself that her heart would heal. Tonight was about Margaret, and she wouldn't spoil her happiness for anything in the world. She doctored her makeup, powdered her nose and jutted her chin as she left the lounge.

Hayes stood like a sentinel outside the doorway, his Stetson pulled low, shading his eyes. "Taylor—"

"Don't," she said sharply. "I'm going to hire a private bodyguard so you can be dismissed immediately."

A sardonic sound echoed from his throat. "You can hire some pretty boy if you want, but I have a job to do here and I'm not leaving until it's done."

She glared at him. "Fine. Just keep your distance."

"Don't worry," he muttered in a low voice.

She brushed past him and rushed into the ballroom, weaving between the guests who were greeting Margaret and Devon and seating themselves for dinner. Hayes followed her, and stood away from the table by a stage area draped in red velvet.

Margaret rose and went toward him, then gestured for him to join them, but he shook his head. Taylor sipped her water, sensing he felt out of place amongst their group, but he really belonged at the table with Margaret. Still, hurt prevented her from insisting he sit and eat with them.

The dinner seemed strained, Devon and Margaret exchanging uncomfortable looks as Kenneth and Tammy joined them. Link claimed his place beside Margaret, his expression stoic. Tammy plastered herself to Kenneth all evening and Devon refused to leave Margaret's side. But Margaret and Kenneth exchanged odd looks occasionally, making Taylor wonder what was going on.

Kenneth even went over and spoke to Hayes—she assumed he was asking about the investigation, but Kenneth seemed more ruffled than usual and tugged at his collar as he returned. Her gaze caught Margaret's and pained emotions flickered across Margaret's face.

Link offered a long-winded toast to Margaret and Devon, and Margaret smiled, although she glanced again at Kenneth. Taylor tensed, something passing between her friend and Kenneth, triggering a distant memory of another time when she'd seen Margaret and Kenneth together, laughing and looking at each other as if they shared something intimate.

She gasped and nearly choked on her water as the truth dawned on her. Was Kenneth the reason Margaret had never married? Had she been in love with him all these years?

Could Kenneth be Hayes's father?

Margaret excused herself to go to the powder room and Taylor followed, well aware that Hayes dogged their movements. But as she'd requested, he maintained his distance.

Just as Taylor pushed at the door to the lounge, a loud noise ripped through the air. God, a bomb!

Taylor screamed as the door shattered, wood and glass splintered and smoke burst from the inside.

Chapter Twenty

Hayes's heart raced as he pushed Margaret and Taylor to the floor. Dammit, someone had just tried to blow them up!

When was this madness going to end?

Smoke poured from the lounge, pieces of wood, tile, glass pelting the outer area. Screams reverberated across the grand entryway, guests running and shouting in horror.

"Taylor, Margaret, are you okay?"

Taylor turned toward him, her face streaked with soot and a line of blood. "I'm all right. Margaret?"

Margaret made a soft moan, and Hayes's breath tightened in his chest as he gently helped her sit up. "I'm fine," she said, although terror streaked her voice and a bruise marred her arm where she'd fallen.

"Was anyone else inside?" he asked.

Taylor shook her head. "I don't know."

He called 9-1-1. "We need an ambulance." He gave the address, then punched in Brody's number and explained what had happened. "Get a crime scene unit here ASAP and I need help questioning the guests."

Link Hathaway, Devon Goldenrod and Kenneth Sutton all stormed toward Taylor and Margaret, concern on their faces as they hovered over the women.

Hayes crossed to the doorway where guests were trying to escape, then held up his hand and shouted. "I'm sorry, folks, but no one is leaving yet. This is a crime scene now. Everyone has to be questioned, so just settle down and relax."

The next two hours were total chaos. Brody and Egan arrived along with two local officers, and they herded the guests back inside the ballroom and divided up to question them.

He, Brody and Egan took the major suspects while the paramedics tended to Margaret and Taylor and CSI searched the lounge. Security for the country club managed to confine the area outside to prevent others from entering or leaving.

Link, Devon and Kenneth stood guard around Margaret and Taylor, while Tammy Sutton hovered nearby, acting concerned, although she looked irritated with the attention her husband was bestowing on the other two women. Goldenrod kept one hand on Margaret's shoulder as if to remind himself that she had survived.

Or that she was his?

Egan joined him as he walked toward the group. He desperately wanted to talk to Taylor and his mother....

His *mother?*

A sharp pang of fear clutched at him. He'd just found her and had almost lost her. And he hadn't even made an attempt to get to know her.

Where did they go from here?

Did he want to try?

Then Taylor's terrified gaze met his, and his heart clenched. He closed the distance between them, needing to verify she was safe.

Remembering the night before when they'd made love, he itched to hold her, but she frowned when he approached as if to remind him of their earlier conversation, that she'd proclaimed her love and he'd thrown it in her face.

Kenneth Sutton edged up beside him, authority in his tone. "What's going on? Do you know who did this?"

"Not yet, but I will," Hayes growled. "I need to speak to each of you alone."

Kenneth frowned, and Link and Devon exchanged annoyed looks. "Margaret, you and Taylor first."

Egan ushered Link aside to question him, and Kenneth and Tammy moved to a sofa nearby, while Brody appeared to interrogate Devon.

"Margaret, Taylor," Hayes said, "did you see anyone leaving the lounge when you got there?"

"No," they both murmured at once.

"Either this attempt was made on Taylor alone and you got caught up in it, Margaret, or someone wanted you out of the way, too. It obviously has something to do with that P.I.'s death."

Margaret clutched Taylor's hands, trembling.

"Who else knows about me?" he asked.

She wet her lips. "Devon, and…this afternoon I told your father."

Hayes's stomach churned. "How did he react?"

"He would never do this, Hayes, I can assure you that." Margaret's voice cracked.

"How did he react, Margaret?"

"He was upset, angry, hurt." Her eyes implored him to believe her. "He insisted that if he'd known, he would have been part of your life, that he would have stood by me. But he was so young and so was I."

"Who is he?" Hayes skimmed the room. "Is he here?"

She hesitated, then nodded and lowered her voice. "Hayes…Kenneth Sutton is your father."

Her declaration echoed in his ears. Kenneth Sutton, the city councilman? The man running for governor?

A man who wouldn't have wanted a kid to stand in his way years ago…or now.

No wonder Margaret hadn't told Kenneth. No wonder she'd shipped him away.

Shock and hurt clouded his thoughts, the pain so intense he thought his chest would explode.

He had to control himself, couldn't let emotions interfere. Had to think like a Texas Ranger.

Which meant Kenneth Sutton had just jumped to the top of his suspect list for this bombing.

Would Sutton kill Taylor and Margaret to keep the truth from being revealed?

Goldenrod also had a lot to lose. He'd been all over Margaret tonight. Had been second in line to Kenneth Sutton for years. Maybe he feared that when the truth finally came out, that Margaret and Kenneth might get together and he'd lose to Sutton again.

TAYLOR HUGGED MARGARET as Hayes strode toward Kenneth.

"He wouldn't do this," Margaret insisted in a pained voice. "Kenneth wouldn't hurt you or me, Taylor. He wants to make amends to Hayes. Said he'd make their relationship public, but he wanted to talk to Hayes first."

"Does Tammy know?" Taylor asked, remembering how she'd clung to Kenneth's side all evening.

"I don't know." Margaret sighed then looked up at Taylor. "What's going on with you and Hayes, Taylor? I thought you two were…maybe involved."

Taylor winced. She'd never been good at hiding her feelings.

"You're in love with him, aren't you?" Margaret asked. "If you are, it's okay, Taylor. I'd like nothing better than to see you with my son."

Taylor sighed. "It doesn't matter, Margaret. He made it clear that he doesn't have feelings for me."

"It's all my fault," Margaret whispered. "I can't blame him for the way he feels about us. He must be so hurt."

Taylor winced. He was hurting, but she was hurt, too. She couldn't go to him tonight or ever again, not after the things he'd said.

A minute later, Hayes returned with Kenneth in tow and escorted the four of them into a private room. Margaret gave Kenneth an apologetic look, but he shrugged it off, watching Hayes as if searching for some semblance of himself.

"Let's lay all the cards on the table," Hayes said dryly. "Mr. Sutton, Margaret just informed me that she told you that you have a son."

Kenneth scrubbed a hand over his chin. "Yes. I swear I didn't know, Hayes."

"Not a clue?" Hayes asked bitterly.

Sutton hesitated. "No. Although…maybe I should have figured it out."

"What do you mean by that?" Hayes asked.

Kenneth paced the room. "A while back, when Kimberly was working for me, she came to me with speculations."

"Kimberly did?" Hayes asked.

"Yes. She claimed that you had a rare blood type, AB Negative. That's also my blood type."

"How did she know your blood type?" Hayes asked.

"She answered the phone for me. I get constant requests to donate blood. Then she saw a picture of me as a kid and thought there was a resemblance between us. Apparently she did some digging on her own and heard gossip that Margaret had given up a child." He whirled around. "But I didn't believe her. I assured her that she was wrong, that if Margaret had given birth, she would have told me. That she would never have kept a secret like that."

Tears trickled down Margaret's cheeks, disbelief and hurt on Kenneth's.

Kenneth dragged his hand down his face. "I thought Kimberly was going to blackmail me so we argued and she left."

"So you hired Montoya to kill her?" Hayes asked.

"No," Kenneth said sharply. "Absolutely not. I would never hurt a person." He stepped closer to Hayes, a muscle ticking in his jaw. "If I'd known about you, I would have married Margaret and been a father to you."

"I couldn't trap you like that," Margaret cried.

"Our son deserved to know us," Kenneth said emphatically. "And we could have made it work, Margaret."

"Yeah, right," Hayes said sarcastically. "Having a kid would have ruined your political aspirations, Sutton.

And now with your bid for the governor's chair…" He paused, and anger flared in Sutton's eyes.

But Hayes continued, "As a last resort, you hired someone to plant a bomb to kill Taylor and Margaret tonight to protect your career."

Kenneth reared back as if Hayes had punched him in the face. "You're wrong. I would never hurt Margaret." He turned a pained look her way. "Never in a million years."

Taylor saw the truth in his eyes then and wondered if Hayes could see it. Kenneth was still in love with Margaret. She wondered if Margaret saw it, too.

Or if Tammy or Devon knew.

If so, one of them might want to get rid of her and Margaret. One of them could have set the bomb.

But Hayes said he had confirmed that Tammy was with Kenneth the night of the pool attack.

Had she lied?

Or could Devon have tried to kill her to stop her from finding the truth?

Chapter Twenty-One

Emotions ran high as Hayes drove Taylor home. Thankfully the medics had released both her and Margaret, but he had to wait until the next day to get the results on the forensics evidence from the bombing. Of course, nearly every female guest at the country club that night had been inside the lounge, so they needed fingerprints on some part of the actual bomb to pinpoint its maker.

She unlocked the door and he followed her in, willing his hands to stay put when what he really wanted to do was drag her into his arms and feel her breath on his cheek, to know that she was safe forever.

"Can I get you something, Taylor?" he asked.

She looked exhausted, her hair was disheveled, her dress stained. But he'd never thought her more beautiful. "I just want to go to bed."

He started to follow her up the staircase, but she waved him off. "Don't, Hayes. Just find out who set off the bomb so we can both get on with our lives."

Her dismissal cut, but she was right.

Still, he didn't sleep at all that night. Kept replaying

the scene where he heard the explosion, where he saw his mother and Taylor both nearly die.

Dammit, he was all tied in knots.

The next morning, he called for the forensics results first thing, but they didn't have them yet. Taylor spent most of the day in her suite, obviously avoiding him. When she finally emerged, she was dressed for the ceremony, although her eyes looked slightly puffy as if she hadn't slept much, either.

They drove in silence to the church for pictures, and he stood to the side, again feeling like an outsider. But today as he watched Margaret, he saw the softness about her, the tender way she treated Taylor, the fear in her eyes that he would never accept her.

He had to forgive her.

But Kenneth...he didn't quite trust that the politician would have sacrificed his life years ago to include him in his family.

"I DON'T KNOW IF I CAN GO through with the wedding." Margaret paced the bride's room. "Last night Devon and I had a terrible argument. He accused me of sneaking behind his back and seeing Kenneth, but that's not true. I've always respected Kenneth's marriage to Tammy. And I wouldn't do anything to jeopardize Kenneth's future."

Taylor thrust a tissue into Margaret's hand, then adjusted her veil. "Because you're in love with him," Taylor said quietly. "You've never stopped loving him, have you, Margaret? That's the reason you stayed single all these years."

Margaret's face fell. "Is it so obvious?"

Taylor shook her head. "No, but you forget you're talking to your best friend here. I saw the way the two of you were looking at each other last night."

"It's such a mess," Margaret cried.

"It's going to be all right," Taylor said.

"How?" Margaret's voice choked. "When I told Kenneth and saw how hurt he was, and then saw him talking to Hayes…"

She gulped back tears. "I'm going to call off the wedding. It's not fair to Devon."

The door squeaked open, and Tammy Sutton appeared in the doorway. Taylor frowned, wondering if Tammy had overheard them.

Then Tammy slid a gun from her purse and pointed it at them, and Taylor had her answer.

"You had to tell Kenneth and ruin everything," Tammy snarled. "But you won't stop this wedding."

Margaret gasped. "You knew?"

Tammy nodded, bitterness lacing her voice when she spoke. "Your father told me years ago. And then Devon phoned to warn me that you were going to tell Kenneth."

Margaret pressed a hand to her chest. "Devon did what?"

Tammy's sinister laugh echoed through the room. "Yes, he wants you, Margaret. Now this is what you're going to do," Tammy said. "You're going to march yourself out there and marry Devon. He loves you, and Kenneth is mine. You and that bastard kid of yours aren't going to ruin our lives and keep him from the governor's chair. Not after all I've done."

She swung the .22 toward Taylor. "This is all your

fault. You had to go nosing into things. You should have stayed out of our business."

"You…you're the one who tried to kill me?" Taylor choked out.

A crazed rage flashed in Tammy's eyes as she nodded. "And if you don't keep quiet, I will shoot you now, Taylor."

Margaret clutched Taylor's hand. "Please don't hurt Taylor."

Tammy nudged her with the gun. "Then let's go. Your fiancé is waiting."

HAYES POSITIONED HIMSELF at the back of the church directly beside the center aisle. The guests had filled in, the church overflowing, the scent of lilies and roses hanging heavily in the air.

The music for the wedding party piped up, and Taylor appeared, then Margaret on her father's arm. He was momentarily mesmerized when he looked at Taylor.

All night he'd craved her, had thought of nothing but crawling into her bed and making love to her again. His body reacted now, hardening, yet fear slipped into the mix. Not a fear of loving her, but a fear of never telling her.

Of losing her forever.

He froze, reality hitting him. He was in love with Taylor.

But what in the hell did he have to offer her?

She started down the aisle, but she was trembling. He frowned, but Hathaway stepped up, and Margaret gave Hayes a strange look, emotions darkening her eyes.

Then the wedding march began, the guests stood and Margaret and Link began their walk down the aisle.

Egan approached him and leaned over, speaking in a low voice. "I just talked to forensics. They found a print on the remainder of that explosive device last night."

His breath stalled in his chest. "Sutton?"

Egan shook his head. "Close, though. His wife, Tammy."

Hayes stiffened, then his gaze swept the room, searching for the couple. Kenneth and Tammy were seated in the third row, the seats on the end by the center aisle. As Taylor walked past her, sweat beaded on Hayes's forehead. He gestured for Egan to move up one side while he took the other. There were too many people here to arrest her now. It was too dangerous.

But just as Taylor took her place at the front of the church, he noticed a pistol in Tammy's hands. She held it hidden beneath her handbag, but pointed toward Margaret.

He had to do something. Stop the wedding and clear everyone out.

Moving silently, he inched toward the front, but Tammy caught his gaze, and pure rage and fury flared on her face. She must have realized his intent, and she shot up from the seat, her expression crazed. "Don't think about it. This wedding will go on."

Gasps and screams echoed through the packed church, and shock reddened Kenneth's face. "Tammy, what in the world is going on?"

She threw a spiteful look his way. "You're mine, Kenneth, and no one is going to take you away or ruin our future."

Kenneth vaulted up and reached for her, but she swung the gun wildly. "No, Kenneth, the wedding has to go on." She rushed into the aisle, waving her hands like a wild woman. "I'll kill everyone here if you try to stop it."

People ducked in their seats, crying and screaming, and she aimed the gun at Margaret.

"Mrs. Sutton," Hayes said calmly, "give me the gun. You don't want to hurt anyone."

She pointed the gun at him, her voice shrill. "You should have stayed out of Cantara Hills."

"It's not his fault," Margaret said. "Please, Tammy, don't hurt him."

Her hand trembled, her eyes twitching, her jerky movements indicating she was out of control. "You whore, you ruined everything!" Then she spun toward Taylor. "And so did you. This is all your fault."

"I didn't hurt anyone," Taylor said.

"You should have minded your own business!" Tammy shouted.

Hayes shielded Margaret and Taylor with his body. "Stop it, Tammy," Hayes said. "You don't want to do this."

"I have to," she cried. "Don't you see, Kenneth, they're ruining everything we've worked for our entire lives."

"You did that when you conspired to kill Taylor and Morris," Hayes said. "How many more people did you kill, Tammy?"

Kenneth's face paled. "My God, Tammy, what have you done?"

"Everything I did I did for us," she screamed.

"Tammy, wait." Kenneth lowered his voice, trying

to reach for the gun. "Give the gun to me and let's talk. I'll help you…."

"No," Tammy shouted. "You know about that bastard kid now. After everything I did to keep it from you. And Devon. For God's sake, Margaret, he wanted you so badly he killed that man Morris to protect your dirty little secret."

Everyone turned toward Devon whose face brightened with anger. "That was an accident," Devon argued. "I only went to pay him off, to keep him from divulging that information, but he fought with me."

Kenneth's eyes widened. "You both knew I had a son and didn't tell me?"

"Of course, I didn't tell you," Tammy screeched, waving the gun toward one of the press as the reporter captured a photograph. The reporter dropped his camera and gestured for her not to shoot, and she wheeled back around on Kenneth.

"Then you would have married her instead of me. And we wouldn't have had our wonderful life."

"Our wonderful life has been a lie," Kenneth barked.

"No…" Tammy said on a ragged cry. "When they're all gone, we can go back to normal."

She was delusional, Hayes thought. Had completely lost her mind.

Tammy's hand trembled as her finger tightened around the gun.

Kenneth vaulted in front of Tammy, shielding Hayes just as the bullet was fired.

Margaret and Taylor screamed as Hayes pushed them out of the line of fire. Kenneth's body bounced backward, then he collapsed to the floor, unconscious, blood pooling on the floor.

THE NEXT FEW HOURS WERE chaotic. Taylor clung to Margaret as the Rangers arrested Devon and Tammy, and the ambulance arrived. "I have to go to the hospital with Kenneth," Margaret said.

Link insisted on driving Margaret, and Hayes and Taylor rushed to his SUV. He flipped on his siren, racing to meet the ambulance as it arrived. The press met them at the hospital, but Hayes ordered security to keep them outside.

The next two hours dragged by in slow motion as Kenneth was rushed to surgery. Victoria and Caroline huddled with Taylor and Margaret, offering comfort.

When Hayes joined them in the waiting room, he stood aside, looking morose and torn over what to do. The doctor appeared and announced that Kenneth needed a transfusion, and Hayes immediately volunteered his blood.

Tears burned Taylor's eyes. Kenneth had saved his son, and now Hayes was going to save his father's life. Maybe somehow, out of all this, the men could be friends.

When he returned, Margaret rushed to him. "Thank you, Hayes. I know this is difficult for you, and I can't tell you what it means to me to have you here."

He nodded and started to speak, but Link approached. "Thank you for saving my daughter's life." He extended his hand.

Hayes stared at it as if unclear what the gesture meant, but shook it. "That's my job."

Her heart ached for him. Hayes looked so out of place, like a lost boy who wanted to belong. But protecting Margaret had been more than a job. She could see

Hayes softening toward her, the concern in his eyes when Tammy had aimed that gun at her. Maybe in time, he and Margaret and Kenneth could develop some kind of a relationship.

She turned away and wrapped her arms around her waist. Only she'd have no place in his life.

HAYES'S CHEST HURT FROM the emotions bombarding him. Fear for Kenneth hit him, though he didn't know why. The man had never done anything for him...except to save his life.

Brody and Egan strode in, and he met them at the door. "That was fast."

"They spilled their guts," Brody said.

Taylor, Margaret and her father hurried over, as well. "Tell us everything," Hathaway said.

"Tammy admitted that she was afraid she'd lost Kenneth and that she had to make sure everyone who knew of Margaret's baby died. She panicked when she found out it was you, Hayes, and that you were in Cantara Hills. She figured it was only a matter of time before the truth came out, so she conspired with Montoya to kill Kimberly. Then she tried to kill Taylor because she'd hired the P.I." He paused. "And Link sent Walt to bribe the P.I., but Devon beat him to it."

"What about Carlson Woodward?" Hayes asked.

"Tammy drugged him, hoping we'd blame everything on him and Montoya," Brody said. "She also knew how much Devon wanted you, Margaret, so she conspired with Devon to keep you from finding out the truth. Only Taylor got in the way. Devon was jealous of Kenneth and stole the sealed bid so Link's company would win the bid on the new city library project, and he'd earn favors with you, Mr. Hathaway." Brody paused again. "Then Tammy made it appear as if Kenneth had stolen the bids so she could trap him into staying with her if he tried to leave her for Margaret. She was going to squeal on Goldenrod."

Margaret looked at Link. "But why did you tell Tammy about my baby?"

Link clenched his jaw. "We had an affair back then. I let it slip."

"So helping you with the bids was payback."

He shrugged.

"It's finally over then?" Taylor asked.

Brody nodded. "Yes. You should be safe now."

The doctor stepped into the doorway and cleared his throat. "Mr. Sutton is in recovery now. It was touch and go and he needs rest, but he should make a full recovery in time."

Margaret twisted her hands together. "Can we see him?"

The doctor peered over bifocals. "Only for a minute. And just one at a time."

Clearly relieved, Margaret hurried behind the doctor. Hayes was Kenneth's son. He should be with him, too. But he remained rooted to the spot.

Brody elbowed Hayes. "Victoria and Caroline are going home together. Egan and I are going for a beer to celebrate putting this one to rest."

Egan seconded it, and Hayes glanced at Taylor, then walked away with the Rangers. Taylor was safe now. He could leave her with her friends.

And he could get the hell out of Cantara Hills and back to the badge.

He'd thought he'd feel excited but all he felt was a deep gaping hole in his chest, along with anguish.

He'd found his real family, but he didn't belong with them any more than he did with Taylor. It was time to let them go.

Chapter Twenty-Two

As soon as they reached the end of the hallway, Brody turned to him. "What in the hell are you doing, Hayes?"

He frowned. "What do you mean?"

"You just found your family. Your mother and father. You need to be with them."

"I don't belong there," Hayes said.

"Why not?" Egan asked. "Because they have money?"

"That's part of it."

"It looked to me like they wanted to mend things. You should give them a chance," Brody said.

"Yeah," Egan said. "Don't cut off your nose to spite your face."

"I don't want anything from them, especially their money," Hayes snapped.

"Maybe. Maybe not. But you want Taylor Landis, so don't let your damn stubborn pride get in the way," Egan said.

Hayes glared at them both. Just because they'd found love they were suddenly experts.

Hayes glanced at Brody, still worried about the tension between them. "About Kimberly…"

"Don't," Brody said. "I've had time to cool down. I know you cared for Kimberly and she did you."

"I did," Hayes said. "She was one of my three best friends."

A silent moment of understanding passed among them where they all acknowledged their love for Kimberly and the fact that they mourned her death. She would always be a part of their disjointed family, a part they'd never forget.

Finally Brody spoke. "I miss Kimberly like crazy, but she would want you to be happy, Hayes. To be with your family." He hesitated, his voice thick. "And with Taylor, if you love her."

"*Is* that what you want?" Egan asked.

Hayes scrubbed his hand over his head, barely able to breathe. "Yes."

"Then get your sorry ass back to her," Brody growled.

Egan clapped him on the back. "Yeah, we'll have that celebratory beer at your wedding."

"I don't know if she'll have me," Hayes admitted. "Not after the things I said."

Brody laughed. "Hell, then get on your knees like a real man and grovel your heart out."

A chuckle rumbled from him. "You're right. Pride is overrated." And Taylor was worth chucking his.

His heart stuttering, he turned on his heels. Taylor had been dead-on in reading him, in understanding him. He'd been the snob, not her. He'd been the coward.

But he'd prove he could change.

And he wouldn't take no for an answer. He was stubborn, and when he wanted something like he'd wanted to be a ranger, he hadn't let anything stand in his way.

Right now he wanted Taylor Landis.

TAYLOR WIPED AT THE TEARS she'd tried not to let fall after Hayes left. Then he suddenly appeared in the doorway, and her breath caught. Before she could ask him why he'd returned, Margaret came back to the waiting room, her eyes red rimmed, her father standing by quietly. "How is he?" Taylor asked.

"He's groggy and in some pain, but coherent." She squeezed Taylor's hand. "He said he loved me, Taylor, that he had all these years. That he didn't blame me for not telling him about the baby, that he had been cocky and full of ambition back then, and knew I'd done what I thought was right." She sniffed. "When this dies down, he wants us to be together."

"What do you want, Margaret?"

"I want to be with him. I've always loved him," Margaret said softly. She turned to Hayes. "And we both want to make it up to you, Hayes, to have a relationship if you'll let us be part of your life."

Emotions strained Hayes's face, and Taylor held her breath until he nodded. She forced a smile and decided it was time for her to leave. She suddenly felt like the stranger, out of place.

"I guess I'll go home now," she said, then hugged her friend. "I'll talk to you later, Margaret."

Margaret nodded, and Hayes took her arm. "Come on, I'll drive you."

"I can call for a car," she said, still hurt.

"No, I'm driving you."

They rode in silence to her estate, and she wondered if perhaps he had more bad news, that the case wasn't really closed.

When they arrived, he asked her to step aside to the pool, making her nerves stretch even thinner.

Taylor paced along the pool edge. "Hayes, what's going on? Is something wrong?"

He nodded. "Yes."

She paused and stared at him. "What?"

"I'm in love with you," he blurted.

She shook her head, uncertain she'd heard him right. "What?"

"I'm in love with you." His voice was stronger now, but heat, desire, other emotions flickered in his eyes.

Hope tickled her, but she remembered what he'd said at the country club and tamped it down. "And that's a problem?"

"Hell, yeah, because I've been an idiot." His voice turned gruff. "I didn't mean to hurt you earlier at the club, but I don't know what I have to offer you." He gestured around the estate. "You already have everything."

"You can give me your love." A soft mellow warmth spread through her, excitement spiking her blood at the same time. "Don't you get it, Hayes? That's all I want, all I need."

His eyes darkened. "Is it enough?"

She nodded, then looped her arms around his neck. "Yes, you big sexy idiot. You're all I've ever wanted in a man."

He tilted his head. "I want to marry you," Hayes said gruffly, "but I don't think I could live at your estate. I won't be a kept man."

She smiled and traced a finger over his badge. She'd known that beneath that badge lay the heart of a loving man. One who'd make a great husband and father. "Me neither. I'd much rather live on your ranch."

His eyes flared with emotions. "You really liked it?"

"I loved it," she declared, then kissed his neck. "Just like I love you. But we might have to make a few changes."

His expression turned wary. "What kind of changes?" He paused. "You want a pool? To get rid of the country furniture? The handmade quilts?"

"No." She threaded her fingers in his hair. "I was thinking we could get a cat to curl up on the rug."

He shrugged. "I'm more of a dog person, but I guess I could live with a cat."

She brushed a kiss along his jaw. "There's something else."

"What?"

"Maybe we could finish one of those upstairs rooms for a nursery."

A smile twitched at his mouth. "You want babies?"

She kissed him again, teasing his mouth with her tongue. "Let's start with just one."

"A little girl," he said in a husky tone.

She unbuttoned the top button of his shirt. "A boy."

He laughed and so did she. They would always have differences but they'd work them out together.

"At least we agree on one thing," he whispered against her ear.

His hard length throbbed against her belly. "That we're made for each other in bed?"

He nibbled at her ear. "Right. I guess we'll just have to spend a lot of time there."

She took his hand and led him inside, then up the stairs to her bedroom. The stars were twinkling through the window, the moon beaming bright, and her heart was overflowing with love.

It was going to be a long and wicked but wonderful life.

* * * * *

Look for Rita Herron's new series
GUARDIAN ANGEL INVESTIGATIONS
*coming in November
from Harlequin Intrigue!*

The Colton family is back!
Enjoy a sneak preview of
COLTON'S SECRET SERVICE by Marie Ferrarella,
part of THE COLTONS: FAMILY FIRST *miniseries.*

Available from Silhouette Romantic Suspense
in September 2008.

He cautioned himself to be leery. He was human and he'd been conned before. But never by anyone nearly so attractive. Never by anyone he'd felt so attracted to.

In her defense, Nick supposed that Georgie could actually be telling him the truth. That she was a victim in all this. He had his people back in California checking her out, to make sure she was who she said she was and had, as she claimed, not even been near a computer but on the road these last few months that the threats had been made.

In the meantime, he was doing his own checking out. Up close and exceedingly personal. So personal he could feel his blood stirring.

It had been a long time since he'd thought of himself as anything other than a law enforcement agent of one type or other. But Georgeann Grady made him remember that beneath the oaths he had taken and his devotion to duty, there beat the heart of a man.

A man who'd been far too long without the touch of a woman.

He watched as the light from the fireplace caressed the outline of Georgie's small, trim, jean-clad body as she moved about the rustic living room that could have easily come off the set of a Hollywood Western. Except that it was genuine.

As genuine as she claimed to be?

Something inside of him hoped so.

He wasn't supposed to be taking sides. His only interest in being here was to guarantee Senator Joe Colton's safety as the latter continued to make his bid for the presidency. Everything else was supposed to be secondary, but, Nick had to silently admit, that was just a wee bit hard to remember right now.

Earlier, before she'd put her precocious handful of a daughter to bed, Georgie had fed his appetite by whipping up some kind of a delicious concoction out of the vegetables she'd pulled from her garden. Vegetables that, by all rights, should have been withered and dried. She'd mentioned that a friend came by on occasion to weed and tend it. Still, it surprised him that somehow she'd managed to make something mouthwatering out of it.

Almost as mouthwatering as she looked to him right at this moment.

Again, he was reminded of the appetite that hadn't been fed, hadn't been satisfied.

And wasn't going to be, Nick sternly told himself. At least not now. Maybe later, when things took on a more definite shape and all the questions in his head were answered to his satisfaction, there would be time to explore this feeling. This woman. But not now.

Damn it.

"Sorry about the lack of light," Georgie said, breaking into his train of thought as she turned around to face him. If she noticed the way he was looking at her, she gave no indication. "But I don't see a point in paying for electricity if I'm not going to be here. Besides, Emmie really enjoys camping out. She likes roughing it."

"And you?" Nick asked, moving closer to her, so close that a whisper would have trouble fitting in. "What do you like?"

The very breath stopped in Georgie's throat as she looked up at him.

"I think you've got a fair shot of guessing that one," she told him softly.

* * * * *

*Be sure to look for COLTON'S SECRET SERVICE
and the other following titles from*
THE COLTONS: FAMILY FIRST *miniseries:*
RANCHER'S REDEMPTION by Beth Cornelison
*THE SHERIFF'S AMNESIAC BRIDE
by Linda Conrad*
SOLDIER'S SECRET CHILD by Caridad Piñeiro
BABY'S WATCH by Justine Davis
A HERO OF HER OWN by Carla Cassidy

Romantic
SUSPENSE

Sparked by Danger,
Fueled by Passion.

The Coltons Are Back!

Marie Ferrarella
Colton's Secret Service

The Coltons: Family First

On a mission to protect a senator, Secret Service agent
Nick Sheffield tracks down a threatening message only
to discover Georgie Gradie Colton, a rodeo-riding single
mom, who insists on her innocence. Nick is instantly
taken with the feisty redhead, but vows not to let his
feelings interfere with his mission. Now he must figure
out if this woman is conning him or if he can trust her
and the passion they share....

Available September wherever books are sold.

Visit Silhouette Books at www.eHarlequin.com   SRS27598

REQUEST YOUR FREE BOOKS!

2 FREE NOVELS PLUS 2 FREE GIFTS!

◆ HARLEQUIN®
INTRIGUE®

Breathtaking Romantic Suspense

YES! Please send me 2 FREE Harlequin Intrigue® novels and my 2 FREE gifts (gifts are worth about $10). After receiving them, if I don't wish to receive any more books, I can return the shipping statement marked "cancel." If I don't cancel, I will receive 6 brand-new novels every month and be billed just $4.24 per book in the U.S. or $4.99 per book in Canada, plus 25¢ shipping and handling per book and applicable taxes, if any*. That's a savings of close to 15% off the cover price! I understand that accepting the 2 free books and gifts places me under no obligation to buy anything. I can always return a shipment and cancel at any time. Even if I never buy another book from Harlequin, the two free books and gifts are mine to keep forever.

182 HDN EEZ7   382 HDN EEZK

Name	(PLEASE PRINT)
Address	Apt. #
City	State/Prov. Zip/Postal Code

Signature (if under 18, a parent or guardian must sign)

Mail to the **Harlequin Reader Service:**
IN U.S.A.: P.O. Box 1867, Buffalo, NY 14240-1867
IN CANADA: P.O. Box 609, Fort Erie, Ontario L2A 5X3

Not valid to current subscribers of Harlequin Intrigue books.

Want to try two free books from another line?
Call 1-800-873-8635 or visit www.morefreebooks.com.

* Terms and prices subject to change without notice. N.Y. residents add applicable sales tax. Canadian residents will be charged applicable provincial taxes and GST. Offer not valid in Quebec. This offer is limited to one order per household. All orders subject to approval. Credit or debit balances in a customer's account(s) may be offset by any other outstanding balance owed by or to the customer. Please allow 4 to 6 weeks for delivery. Offer available while quantities last.

Your Privacy: Harlequin is committed to protecting your privacy. Our Privacy Policy is available online at www.eHarlequin.com or upon request from the Reader Service. From time to time we make our lists of customers available to reputable third parties who may have a product or service of interest to you. If you would prefer we not share your name and address, please check here. ☐

HI08R